Re-reading *Harry Potter and the Deathly Hallows*

Dr. Graeme Davis

Nimble Books LLC

Contents

Re-reading Harry Potter and the Deathly Hallows

Re-reading "Harry Potter and the Deathly Hallows" is a book of literary criticism of J.K. Rowling's book *Harry Potter and the Deathly Hallows*. It is about the novel, not the films. Inevitably as a work of literary criticism it contains plot spoilers. It is anticipated that enthusiasts for the Harry Potter novels may read this book alongside a re-reading of *Harry Potter and the Deathly Hallows*.

The Need for Literary Criticism

For a book which has enjoyed the massive sales of *Harry Potter and the Deathly Hallows* (15,000,000 copies in the first twenty-four hours alone) there has been very little literary criticism published. Much of what has been written is in the form of very short articles, or on-line material often without an acknowledged author. Neither are really satisfactory. This book is a contribution to the literary criticism of *Harry Potter and the Deathly Hallows*.

The leading critics of our age had a hard task in responding to *Harry Potter and the Deathly Hallows*. Most leading critics work for newspapers, magazines or television channels, and usually these critics have sight of a novel a week or two before publication, and therefore have time to read it, reflect on it and then write their reviews in time for publication day. Yet such was the concern about possible prepublication leaks of *Harry Potter and the Deathly Hallows* that this courtesy was not extended to the critics. They got the book when everyone else got it.

Clearly this is a problem. The book is almost 200,000 words —a doorstop size. Yet the requirement of the major newspapers was for their critics to post a review within hours of publication of the book. Most managed to get something into print, but they did this by exploiting two tried and tested time-saving techniques. One of these, the multi-reader approach, is to have a number of readers each reading a section of the novel, summarizing it and commenting on just their section, and for the lead critic to write the review based on the notes produced by a team or perhaps half a dozen readers. The other technique, the generic approach, is to have much of the review article pre-written on the basis of previous books, with a view to slotting in appropriate phrases when the book has been overviewed (not read) by the reviewer. Of course neither technique—multi-reader or generic—leads to quality reviews. Yet these reviews are the "official" ones and they remain the most quoted. Their publication in leading newspapers and magazines means that they are an appropriate source for the online encyclopedia Wikipedia, and such is the success of Wikipedia as the first port of call for anyone writing on Harry Potter (or just about anything else) that they have become the best known responses. All in all it is rather a shame—the now famous reviews are in fact the poorly researched ones produced within a very few hours of publication. The considered views of people who have actually read and reflected on the novel scarcely get a look in.

Unfortunately we've seen very little in the way of subsequent reviews from professional literary critics. The newspapers seem mostly to have felt they had done their review with their initial response and haven't had a second crack, a big shame as they employ some of the leading critics of our age. Additionally the Harry Potter phenomenon has not generated the volume of literary criticism of (for example) the Dan Brown novels (particularly *The Da Vinci Code*), perhaps because the assiduous efforts of the publishers of Rowling to maintain her intellectual copyright may have had the effect of discouraging some criticism where critics may risk straying from an academic discipline into a possible infringement of the intellectual copyright asserted. Right now as critic response we have the first impressions from the newspapers, and not much else. For a novel as well-read as *Harry Potter and the Deathly Hallows* this is disappointing.

The generic style of review comments may be seen in *The Times*' review (by Alice Fordham): "Rowling's genius is not just her total realization of a fantasy world, but the quieter skill of creating characters that bounce off the page, real and flawed and brave and lovable." Surely this is correct, and surely it applies to every one of the Harry Potter novels, not just this last one. The *New York Times* (Michiko Kakutani) tells us Harry is a hero but also a character we can relate to—indeed true, and true in all the books. There's also comment on the Harry Potter phenomenon rather than on the book—*Time* magazine noted that the publications shows that books are still a mass medium. Several reviewers comment on the plot density of *Harry Potter and the Deathly Hallows*—for example Elizabeth Hand suggests "an entire trilogy's worth of summing-up has been crammed into one volume." There was much speculation before publication that *Harry Potter and the Deathly Hallows* would be dense as there is a lot of plot to be concluded from the series (not of course a trilogy of three books but in fact seven). In a second review published in *The Times* (by Amanda Craig) we are told that Rowling is "not an original, high-concept author," but that nonetheless she is "right up there with other greats of children's fiction"—Craig goes on to comment on how the Harry Potter series has become part of the life of a whole generation of children. From *The Guardian* (Catherine Bennett) we hear that "as her critics say, Rowling is no Dickens." Quite which critics these are I'm not sure as they are not named. We also hear that Rowling has created "in every book, legions of new characters."Actually I'm not sure that this is correct—the characters in the early books are relatively sparse, and none of the books seems to have too many new faces—but it does seem typical of the generic approach of broad comments forced on reviewers by unrealistic time constraints.

By contrast *The Baltimore Sun* (Mary Carole McCauley) noted the straightforward prose of the book—surely not something most review readers are particularly interested in, but something that can be gleaned from a section-by-section reading.

The Christian press struggled to enthuse in its reviews. For example *The Christian Science Monitor* (reviewer Jenny Sawyer) does manage some positives, but also says "... puberty aside, Harry doesn't change much. As envisioned by Rowling, he walks the path of good so unwaveringly that his final victory over Voldemort feels, not just inevitable, but hollow."I'm puzzled! This is not a coming-of-age novel. Harry does not, in fact, walk the path of good "unwaveringly"—one of the most affecting scenes in the entire series is Harry's very human fear and sadness as he walks to what he knows is his certain death at the hands of Voldemort. And Harry's victory is far from inevitable, and his survival a surprise to him, at least. In the penultimate chapter we think he is dead, while in the final chapter he still seems hopelessly out-gunned by Voldemort.

In a nutshell the reviews that don't merely disappoint, they are frequently abysmal in quality. They do no favors to the centuries old art of literature criticism honed at the great universities of the UK and USA.

Re-reading "Harry Potter and the Deathly Hallows"

This book is offered to the thoughtful reader of *Harry Potter and the Deathly Hallows* as a stimulus to thought. Inevitably readers of the book will agree with much and disagree with much that is written here—that is the nature of literary criticism—but the process of agreeing and disagreeing develops a more considered critical response.

Harry Potter and the Deathly Hallows deserves a careful response, more than has been offered by the immediate newspaper views. In my view it has the following characteristics:

- It is a polished work by a highly skilled writer.
- It offers as much to adult readers as to young adults and children. As such it has the potential to become a classic.

- It has become part of global culture.
- It is an outstanding, Christian novel.

Making Sense of the Title: Harry Potter and the Deathly Hallows

No one really knows what the title means. It just doesn't make sense in English, though it does sound sinister and intriguing. Rowling called her first novel *Harry Potter and the Philosopher's Stone*, putting a language conundrum in the title. Her American publisher, Scholastic, would not accept this and forced the change in America to *Harry Potter and the Sorcerer's Stone*. In this final book Rowling has again presented readers with a language puzzle. Just as she thought the children who read her first book were up to the challenge of a difficult title, so Rowing feels that the young adults and adults who read her last book can cope with a challenge. Rowling is undoubtedly expecting a lot of her readers, but maybe readers like this. Of course it is possible to skim over the title without thinking too much about it, but *re-reading* the book is probably time to sort it out. So just what might the title mean?

The verb *to hallow* has very restricted use in English. It can in theory be used with the meaning *to make holy* or *sacred*, but today it is rarely actually used in this context. Instead it is found almost solely in just one place, the Lord's Prayer: "hallowed be Thy name." It is very hard to see how anyone today could use the verb without an implied reference to the Lord's Prayer.

But of course Rowling does not use it as a verb; rather she makes it play the part of a noun. And this is weird! There was once such a noun in English, both in Anglo-Saxon and in Middle English, but that's at least five hundred years ago, and in many cases a thousand years or more. Over the centuries the noun *a hallow* has changed both pronunciation and spelling and it has also changed its part of speech, being used not as a straightforward noun but as part of a noun phrase—in short it has become the adjective *holy*. Sometimes the noun it qualifies is short of meaning, as *a holy thing* or *a holy man*, so *holy* in compounds still approaches the status of a noun. It also crops up today as an etymological part of Halloween (the *holy eve* before All Saints' Day).

Strictly speaking "deathly hallows" means absolutely nothing in Modern English. It sounds as if it should mean something, but it really doesn't. If you struggle for a meaning (which must be what Rowling wants us to do), if you look back to Old English and Middle English and assume that these forms are still valid in English (a bookish concept, though some academics might argue it) then you get *a thing made holy by death*. This does indeed seem to be what Rowling intended. When translators (understandably) queried what "deathly hallows" meant she gave an alternative title for the book: *Harry Potter and the Relics of Death*. This is the title that has been translated into many languages, as for example *Harry Potter et les Reliques de la Mort* (French); *Harry Potter y las Reliquias de la Muerte* (Spanish). Occasionally the translation is as "talisman," as *Harry Potter e os Talismãs da Morte* (Portuguese), and it seems that Rowling found such an alternative meaning to be acceptable also.

Within the book the meaning of "deathly hallows" is of course explained—the items created by Death himself (or perhaps by three clever wizards) which together give control over death. If they are relics of Death—and that is Rowling's translation—then they imply that Death can be conquered. At first this seems to go against Rowling's self-imposed limitation to the magic world she creates, that death in the magic world (as in ours) is absolute and people cannot come back from death. However within the context both of this final book and the Harry Potter series, the message is that there is a life after death, though it is not a life where people truly come back to our world. Thus the many ghosts of Hogwarts have just a shadowy existence; Sirius Black is briefly seen "beyond the veil"; Lily & James Potter, though dead, can help their son; Dumbledore can communicate from beyond the grave (through his portrait); and Harry himself undergoes a near-death experience.

Chapter-by-Chapter Themes

Rowling planned her books chapter by chapter, as has been revealed by some of her rough notes which have come into the public domain. Chapters are meaningful units within the Harry Potter novels. Typically each chapter is of a similar length, has a clear focus with some supporting plot elements, and tends to showcase two or more of the characters, or develop a dynamic between two characters.

Chapter titles in *Harry Potter and the Deathly Hallows* are carefully crafted. As the book is not published with a contents page listing the chapters by name, it is easy to overlook these, but as with so much of Rowling' word-craft they repay more attention.

For example "The Dursleys Departing" uses a ponderous alliterating D sound which fits the overweight Dursleys (at least Mr Dursley and Dudley) and their labored transition into exile. Theirs is no swift and noble exit but an event marked by their distrust of Harry (and everyone else), their vacillation, and a sense that they have become parcels transported by the magic world. "The Life and Lies of Albus Dumbledore" picks up the title of Rita Skeeter's biography. Of course it is usually "life and times"—the substitution of "lies" within the anticipated phrase emphasizes the word lies—Skeeter's book and the chapter are by implication about Dumbledore's lies.

Rowling is keen in the chapter titles to tell us not what happens in a chapter but what they are actually about. In grammatical terms all but two of the chapter title are noun phrases. Chapters 24 of the 36 even start with "the." There is just one complete sentence with both noun and verb phrase (12. "Magic Is Might") and one adverbial phrase (2. "In Memoriam"—though this is probably a quotation). Additionally the first chapter name follows a noun phrase with an adjectival phrase "The Dark Lord Ascending."

Implicit Divisions?

At 200,000 words or thereabouts, *Harry Potter and the Deathly Hallows* is a l-o-n-g book. It appears practical to think of it in terms of three parts, though these are not set out in the book.

Part one (chapters 1—12) shows Harry, Ron, Hermione and the whole Order of the Phoenix as victims. Events are happening around them with little control. While they do plan to guard Harry their plans go wrong. His evacuation from Privet Drive is bodged —leading to a death and a serious injury—while his place of safety at the Weasleys' home is compromised when the Ministry falls. All the characters are driven by events with little sign of planning. Additionally there's a lot of background in this section, things like Dumbledore's will and Kreacher's tale.

Part two (chapters 13—24) shows a counter-attack by Harry, Ron and Hermione—assisted by such unlikely characters as Snape, Kreacher and Dobby. This is the section which sees the first of the outstanding horcruxes sought out and destroyed, and introduces the hallows.

Part three (chapters 25—36) takes us to Hogwarts, the scene of most of the action of the previous six books. The Harry Potter novels could end nowhere else—indeed Rowling is bold to take so much of the final book away from the set all readers have come to know.

About this Re-Reading

The Star System

Every reader has parts of a book that they like more than others. In re-reading *Harry Potter and the Deathly Hallows* I have sought to draw attention to the relative strengths of each. The system measures the chapters one against the other. A ★ (one star) Rowling chapter is probably much better than the best of another author, but may still disappoint Harry Potter fans.

This is for a chapter that isn't of the high standards we have come to expect from Rowling. Inevitably many readers will disagree, but I've held to my views and suggested that in terms of literary style there is a chapter that merits this lowest of star ratings.

★★

This is a chapter which disappoints, usually for reasons which can be set out in terms of a literary style which is less good than that usual for Rowling.

★★★

This is a solid and satisfying Rowling chapter. There are lots of these.

★★★★

This is a particularly good Rowling chapter. There are lots of these too.

★★★★★

This is an outstanding Rowling chapter. In an excellent book there are quite a few of these.

First Reading

Most readers only read a book once, and it is the first reading that matters. Most of Rowling's chapters do have a clear message which should be communicated with just the first reading.

Re-Reading

The Harry Potter novels deserve a second reading, especially *Harry Potter and the Deathly Hallows*. It is on re-reading that many of the details which make the book special are fully noticed. Usually a re-reading deepens the first impressions readers take from a first reading, but on occasions the re-reading modifies significantly what the reader first thought.

Heroes and Villains

Many chapters have a clear hero and a clear villain. Rowling is certainly not "painting by numbers"—she's far too sophisticated a writer for this—yet readers can be alert to the existence in many chapters of a person who acts well, in effect as the hero, and one who acts badly, as the villain. Harry is often hero, occasionally the villain.

Readers are encouraged to commend right action, wherever it is found.

The Secret Life of Severus Snape

Rowling utilizes the plot device of a "back plot." The clearest example in the Harry Potter novels is in *Harry Potter and the Chamber of the Secrets* where it is possible to work out chapter-by-chapter what Ginny Weasley did, though very little of this activity is directly shown in the book. Rowling must have planned it out before writing the book. *Harry Potter and the Deathly Hallows* has a similar "back plot," this one around the activities of Severus Snape. We can piece these together in most chapters.

Snape the double-agent inevitably has two lives. In *Harry Potter and the Half Blood Prince* we see the life he leads at Hogwarts and as a member of the Order of the Phoenix, and get just a glimpse of his life as a Death Eater. In *Harry Potter and the Deathly Hallows* the situation is reversed. Readers believe him to be a loyal supporter of Voldemort. The first chapter sees him playing a key role in Voldemort's meeting. Readers can see no way in which his double agent role can be continuing. It is almost shocking on re-reading the book to find that throughout the story there are clear hints of his true role, hints which most readers miss. Snape indeed has a secret life. His actions in this final book of the Harry Potter story transforms him from apparent murderer into the man Harry comes to regard as one of the bravest men who ever lived.

The Preface

Aeschylus, The Libation Bearers

This is a high-brow reference!

UK universities often teach a Greek play in translation as a first year course within degrees in Arts, particularly Literature and Languages. It is possible that *The Libation Bearers* was on the syllabus for Rowling's Languages degree at University of Exeter. Equally it is quite possible that she has chosen to read it for the fun of it—for Greek drama is richly satisfying and well worth reading.

The play dates from 458BC or thereabouts and is a tragedy around the idea of revenge. On the one hand is the idea of the blood feud, where a crime must be revenged, and a consequence of this obligatory revenge is that the act of revenge creates the motive for another act of obligatory revenge. On the other hand is the idea of civil law, that a crime can be punished and that's the end of the matter. The first is associated with the Furies, some of the oldest deities in the Greek pantheon, while the second is associated with Apollo. In the Athens of Aeschylus the old order was being replaced by the primacy of law, within a society that was the world's first democracy.

The chorus works in Greek plays predominantly as a commentator, in *The Libation Bearers* forwarding the concept of justice. The quotation used by Rowling evokes the horror of the times, calls on the gods for help, and asserts "bless the children, give them triumph now." In order to see that this quote is appropriate I think we need to infer that Rowling regards the heroes of *Harry Potter and the Deathly Hallows* as children. She does of course make age 17 the age of adulthood in her Harry Potter universe, yet I'm not sure that she has herself accepted this—Harry, Ron and Hermione are to her still children. The Battle of Hogwarts of course includes many who are under 17 and by any classification still children. The great battle against Voldemort, the battle against the ideas which Aeschylus characterized as the world of revenge and the Furies, is fought and won by children. After the defeat of Voldemort the children will go on to build a better society

William Penn, More Fruits of Solitude

Again a solid reference!

William Penn (1644-1718) is remembered in America as the founder of the state of Pennsylvania, as well as the city of Philadelphia. In Britain as well as in America he is remembered as one of the early Quakers, the name of the Christian group also called The Religious Society of Friends. In the quotation in the "Preface" we read "Death is but crossing the world, as friends do the seas." Penn is creating an image of death as parallel to a trans-Atlantic crossing. In his day the people who left the British Isles bound for America did so in the knowledge that they were most unlikely to see their family and friends ever again. For those left behind as well as to those who left, a migration to America must have seemed to as a sort of death. Yet to Penn—as to Rowling—the dead are "immortal." Death is no more frightening than a migration.

Rowling's decision to quote a leading Quaker writer is presented without context. In her quotation she uses "friends" with a small "f", where most Quakers would use "Friends" with a capital "F" (or even "Ffriends" with two "Ff"s!) to mean Quaker. She is not a Quaker, and as far as I know has no special links with Quakers or knowledge of Quakers. Yet in the Harry Potter novels she presents a morality of engagement with the world and an outlook of seeing good in others which is about as Quakerly as can be. The life of Harry Potter, without religious denomination and without sacrament, is the life of a Quaker. I think it is unintentional, yet in the actions of Harry Potter, Rowling has presented an ideal Quaker. Her choice of William Penn's text in her "Preface" is certainly appropriate. And the readers who applaud Harry Potter's actions and his faith without dogma might even be Quakers without knowing it!

1. The Dark Lord Ascending

★★★★★

Assessment

This is a chapter that no reader will forget, for Voldemort's council is a Gothic horror. Leading members of his team sit around the table in varying degrees of terror while a prisoner wails in "misery and pain" in a cellar beneath. Around the table Pettigrew is in such fear that he sits so low in his chair he can scarcely be seen. Lucius Malfoy is humiliated and threatened, his son Draco indulged. Above the table Charity Burbage is suspended in a magical cage, soon to be killed in front of the assembly and fed to Voldemort's snake, Nagini. Few authors could paint such an extreme scene without their story appearing ridiculous. The power of Rowling's writing is such that she pulls it off creating an effective and shocking start to the novel. A chapter which could so easily have been a failure is in fact an outstanding success.

Re-Reading

All of the "bad guys" in this chapter can be viewed as having redeeming features. The reader can even feel sorry for them as they experience fear and humiliation and witness an horrific murder. By contrast Voldemort is presented without any possible redeeming features. Rowling is showing us the face of evil.

Heroes and Villains

This is the villains' chapter, with most of the bad guys gathered around a table. Charity Burbage and the Malfoy family are the most obvious victims, though most around the table would seem to wish to be somewhere else. But being a victim doesn't make them heroes. Snape of course performs his double agent role, though is unable to prevent the murder of Charity Burbage. He's impressive, but here hardly a hero. This chapter is atypical in that it does not have a hero.

The Gender Issue

There is an argument that Rowling perpetuates gender stereotypes. Most of the powerful roles go to men. There are however only a few occasions when there is quantitative evidence to explore this assertion. One is here, another is in Chapter Four ("The Seven Potters"). In both locations we get a full list of people who fill a certain role.

Here the named members of the powerful people at Voldemort's meeting are:

- Voldemort
- Severus Snape
- Yaxley
- Lucius Malfoy
- Narcissa Malfoy

- Draco Malfoy
- Dolohov
- Peter Pettigrew
- Bellatrix

Of these Narcissa Malfoy is not actually a Death Eater. She is there in the two traditionally feminine roles of wife and host—wife of Death Eater Lucius, and house-wife who looks after Malfoy Manor where Voldemort is staying. She is introduced as Lucius's wife and she contributes nothing to the meeting. Taking her out the list leaves just eight people. In a world of gender equality there should be four men and four women, but in fact there are seven men and just one woman, Bellatrix. Clearly there is an imbalance here! Bellatrix seems to regard herself as Voldemort's most loyal follower. Rowling dances round the edge of her attraction to Voldemort and it is not ever made explicit, but her near-worship of Voldemort seems a sexual attraction. Rowling presents here a male-dominated world.

The one other woman present is the victim, Charity Burbage, a Hogwarts teacher, though not one whom readers have previously seen. She is seen begging Snape to intercede for her, and dying in a gruesome fashion, hardly heroic roles.

On the basis of this meeting it does seem that Rowling associates power in organizations with men. But an important counterargument is that the single most important theme of the series is the protective and transforming power of maternal love.

The Problem of Evil

Voldemort's council is attended by bad men and women—yet not all are evil. The same list that suggests an implicit view on gender in organizations also gives evidence of an implicit view on evil.

In the course of the book readers discover that not all these members of Voldemort's inner circle are evil. Snape is the double agent who aids Harry by providing incomplete information about the removal (leaving out the ruse of the seven Harry Potters), in the destruction of the horcruxes (by providing the Sword of Gryffindor) and ultimately by providing Harry with the information he needs at the time when he needs it. Ultimately we perceive Snape's bravery, and the goodness of the latter years of his life. Peter Pettigrew repays Harry's mercy (in *Harry Potter and The Prisoner of Laban*) by hesitating to kill him, suggesting a character not wholly evil. Narcissa Malfoy lies to Voldemort (claiming Harry Potter is dead though she knows he is not), revealing her love for her son and her essential decency. Lucius Malfoy does not actively support Voldemort while by the "Epilogue" his son Draco Malfoy has in effect gone over to the other side. Voldemort is of course evil, and most likely three others: Yaxley, Dolohov and Bellatrix.

Of the inner circle of nine bad guys perhaps only four—less than half—are actually evil.

The Secret Life of Severus Snape

Dumbledore has been keen to present Snape as brave for his double agent role, and in this chapter we see just why. Snape is playing the part of one of the Death Eaters most loyal to Voldemort. A man who is fundamentally decent must appear to approve the horrors of Voldemort's meeting. He also has the near-impossible task of frustrating Voldemort's actions without exposing himself.

Snape plays a high-risk game in telling Voldemort the correct date for the transfer of Harry. He trusts that the ruse of the seven Harry Potters will be enough to safeguard Harry. The alternative would have been to allow Voldemort to believe the false trail of the transfer. Yet the result would have been similar. Voldemort would doubtless have sentinels, and whenever Harry was transferred Voldemort and many Death Eaters could be called very quickly indeed. All that the transfer party would gain from Snape's silence on the date is a very few seconds. Snape calculates that these seconds can be given so that his cover is made more secure, and so that he will be one of the Death Eaters on the spot potentially able to help Harry.

In the event Harry is very nearly caught by Voldemort, while the Order of the Phoenix endure a death and a serious injury. Snape's decision has consequences. Would an additional few seconds have avoided Moody being killed? Probably not, but Snape must wonder if the consequences would have been different has his decision been different. His double agent role is a moral conundrum.

The white peacock in this chapter is a striking detail. Many big houses in Britain do keep peacocks in their grounds as these Indian birds adapt well to the British climate and are undeniably impressive. There is an extensive mythology around peacocks, and the rare white peacocks have specific associations attached to them. While the peacock with the splendid eye pattern in its tail feathers represents the all-seeing church, the white peacock additionally represents purity, specifically the purity of the Church. It is hard to be sure whether Rowling is consciously using a Christian symbol or whether she is simply evoking an image of good living in an English manor house. We are told that the white peacock is on top of a yew hedge, a tree associated with English parish churchyards, which does tend to suggest a religious association. I'm inclined to believe that the white peacock is deliberate, introducing a subtle Christian reference even in a scene dominated by Voldemort's evil.

Malfoy Manor is a building of a sort familiar in the English countryside. Once every village in England had its manor house, and while the passage of time has seen some fall into dereliction, many thousands remain, most as private homes. Malfoy Manor—outside hedges, gardens and gravel drive, inside stone floors and marble fireplaces—feels thoroughly English. The white peacocks in the grounds are an unusual touch, but by no means unknown.

The Surname Malfoy does not appear to be part of the British name stock, but it is clearly French in origin, one of the group of surnames which are claimed to be Norman French from the time of William the Conqueror. Rowling does not give us overt background on the Malfoy family, yet the snippets we have suggest a family with a pedigree approaching a thousand years living in the comfort of an inherited home. The environment fits the "pure blood" Malfoy family.

2. *In Memoriam*

Assessment

Sorry JKR, you can do better than this chapter! This is the bits and pieces chapter. We have an incident where Harry cuts his hand on a cup, which doesn't seem particularly relevant for anything at all, and a flash back to Harry's conversation with Dumbledore years ago about the Mirror of Erised, something which adds almost nothing to the story. The bulk of the chapter is the two obituaries of Dumbledore, and they can both be heavy going for readers. Doge's style is stodgy, self-important and self-centered ("I met Dumbledore at the age of eleven … When Albus and I left Hogwarts, we intended to take the then traditional tour of the world together … I shall miss his friendship"); by contrast Skeeter's interview has more life in its language but actually says very little of importance :"I'm not giving away all the highlights".

Re-Reading

The redeeming feature of the chapter is that it deals with a key theme of the book around the nature of reputation. It does indeed prompt thought, but I'm not sure that readers want much deep thought as early as chapter two.

I could be tempted to use the two obituaries as material for a classroom "compare and contrast" activity for English language students—if of course I could get permission.

Heroes and Villains

Harry is the hero of the book and by default the hero of this chapter. Dumbledore is the villain who hasn't left Harry with the information he needs, and whose troubled youth results in a worrying obituary.

Compare and Contrast

Every teacher (and student) knows the activity: compare and contrast two texts describing the same event. This chapter presents two obituaries of Professor Dumbledore, one by Elphias Doge, a long term friend, one by Rita Skeeter, a journalist looking for sensation. The first is a eulogy to a man "with great humanity and sympathy"; the second a character assassination of a man "who dabbled in the Dark Arts" and whose family is a "dungheap." The two presentations are complete opposites.

As far as I can see there are no factual inaccuracies in either story, at least as far as they relate to Dumbledore. I think there is a minor inaccuracy in Skeeter's comment that Harry had a "troubled adolescence" suggesting psychological illness—this was a false story that Skeeter once published about Harry, and which resulted in Hermione imprisoning her as a bug in a jam-jar. Skeeter may well have felt just a little unhappy about her treatment at the hands of

Hermione, and her renewed dig at Harry is perhaps to be expected. Yet this detail is but a minor point in her account. Overall both obituaries manage to tell the story of Dumbledore's life without offense to the truth, yet each is selective in the information they present. Both tell the truth, but not the whole truth. At the wedding Auntie Muriel comments that Doge "skated over the sticky patches", and this is the case. By contrast Doge calls Skeeter a "vulture," preying on the corpse of a dead man, also true.

From a British perspective, the Doge obituary fits the respectable pages of a broadsheet newspaper, perhaps *The Telegraph*. Skeeter's lively interview is more sensational, more appropriate for a magazine.

The Secret Life of Severus Snape

In their obituaries neither Doge nor Skeeter pick up on Dumbledore's friendship with Snape. Skeeter does mention that he was present at Dumbledore's death, though the reference is purely factual.

Dumbledore and Snape's friendship is of seventeen years duration and has resulted in Snape being Dumbledore's only true confidant. Snape has been the true executor of Dumbledore's last wishes, for his murder of Dumbledore is on Dumbledore's instructions, with the intention of saving the soul of Draco Malfoy. Throughout *Harry Potter and the Deathly Hallows* it is Snape who carries forward Dumbledore's plan. Every one of the teachers at

Hogwarts and every member of the Order of the Phoenix knew of this friendship and of the trust Dumbledore put in Snape, yet both Doge and Skeeter chose to ignore it. Perhaps Doge sees the trust as misplaced, and therefore the friendship as better ignored; perhaps Skeeter recognizes that Snape is now applauded by the new order and does not want to offend him by linking him with Dumbledore. The result is that the Dumbledore obituaries, although being opposites in their assessment of Dumbledore, both miss the key friendship which defined the last years of his life and which exemplifies his most laudable quality, his willingness to see the best in everyone.

***British* Pound Cake**—as eaten by Rita Skeeter and her interviewer—is made from one pound of flour, one pound of sugar, one pound of butter and eight 2oz eggs (i.e. a pound of eggs). Frequently ingredients are scaled down—the key is that the proportion is 1:1:1:1. When old-fashioned balance scales were the norm, the eggs were used as the weight to measure the other ingredients. All that remains is to add a pinch of salt. The resulting cake is rich and dense. The term *Pound Cake* is found in America, but the American cake mix is usually modified to create a lighter cake, frequently fruit or lemon zest is added, and often the cake is layered with a filling. *British* Pound Cake—presumably as served by Rita Skeeter—is solid.

Alfred, Lord Tennyson ***In Memoriam AHH*** is surely reflected in the title of this chapter, one of Lord Tennyson's best known poem. It is hard to imagine that she would have been unaware of this. Lord Tennyson's poem is a meditation on the death of his best friend—in many respects the poem says what Harry would have liked to have seen written about Dumbledore. The best known stanza reads:

> I hold it true, whate'er befall;
> I feel it when I sorrow most;
> 'Tis better to have loved and lost
> Than never to have loved at all.

Harry, like Tennyson, has loved and lost.

3. The Dursleys Departing

★★★★

Assessment

There's a chapter such as this in every one of the Harry Potter novels. We see Harry at home with his aunt and uncle in an environment where he endures a lot of abuse from them, mostly with very little protest. Throughout the series there is a change in the relationship between the two. In *Harry Potter and the Philosopher's Stone* (US *Harry Potter and the Sorcerer's Stone*) Harry is dependent on his foster parents—as any eleven year old would be—yet by this the final novel the relationship has turned round so that it is the Dursleys who are dependent on Harry and the support of Harry's magic world for their survival. The power in the relationship has shifted, yet the Dursleys' rudeness remains. Readers enjoy the familiar genre of Harry-at-home, enjoy the blustering Vernon and the spoilt Dudley, and enjoy too the discomfort of the Dursleys. A fun chapter!

Re-reading

Dudley Dursley has not had a particularly good press throughout the Harry Potter novels. In the first he is a figure of fun, with a pig's tail inflicted on him by Hagrid. Later we see that he is a bully. Dumbledore criticizes his parents for their abuse in alloying him to become obese, though mostly readers are encouraged to see Dudley as greedy, spoilt, and therefore responsible for his own shortcomings.

The parting of ways of Harry and the Dursley family was never going to be happy. The Dursleys are going into hiding, expecting that for a long while they will not see their friends and family, and utterly dependent on the magical world they despise. Their life is totally disrupted through no fault of their own. Indeed their predicament is due to their action in providing a home for Harry. However poor that home was it was still an act of charity, and the magical protection invoked works only because of the special relationship that exists between Petunia and Harry, the nephew her sister Lily died for. When in *Harry Potter and The Prisoner of Azkaban* Harry runs away from home after inflating his aunt, the Minister for Magic comments that "deep down" Harry and the Dursleys must love one another. The comment seems wrong at the time uttered, yet within the unhealthy mix of emotions between Harry and the Dursleys, among the dislike, abuse and resentment, there is some element of love.

Vernon Dursley almost shakes Harry's hand, but fails "unable to face it." Harry feels Petunia Dursley "wanted to say something to him." In a different world, a different book, there would have been time and space for the Dudley family and Harry to come to understand the stresses and strains of Dumbledore's imposition of the fostering of Harry on an unwilling family, and come to realize that both had had a lot to put up with. Yes Harry was abused in being forced in his early years to use the cupboard under the stairs as his bedroom and by the unequal treatment of him and Dudley. Yet the Dursleys have had a lot to put up with. At the start of every book we hear of an encounter with the magical world which must be traumatic to the Dursley family. No wonder they want nothing to do with it!

Dudley's words of farewell to Harry are worth noting, not because they are eloquent (they're not!) but because they reveal genuine feeling: "I don't think you're a waste of space … You saved my life." Harry comprehends the unspoken meaning: "coming from Dudley that's like 'I love you'".

Heroes and Villains

The good guy of this chapter is Dudley, who tries to be nice to Harry and tries to express his appreciation of the cousin who saved his life. Harry doesn't come across particularly well. Yes he is provoked by the Dursleys, but he is rude and abrasive.

The Secret Life of Severus Snape

Snape must know about the plan for the Dursleys' departure, just as he knows about the plan for Harry's departure—after all it is ultimately Snape who thought up the scheme. And of course he must know—as Harry does—that Voldemort would like to capture the Dursleys in order to torture them into revealing Harry's whereabouts or use them as hostages that Harry might come to rescue.

Yet the Dursleys' departure is smooth. Snape has not betrayed them.

House Prices are a UK preoccupation that this chapter touches on. Vernon notes that prices are "sky-rocketing." And for most of the post-war years in the UK this has been the case.

The Dursleys live in Surrey, the county that is the most affluent in the UK and a very short commute to the City of London. London—and the whole South East of England—is a part of the world where space for residential property has just about run out. Much land has laws which prohibit building, while elsewhere there are restrictions on the permitted density, ruling out high-rise developments. Yet in the post-war years the population of London and the South East has more than doubled, families expect more living space than did previous generations, and London has established its place as one of the world's leading financial cities. Prices are eye-wateringly high. Think high and go up a bit higher!

There is a long tradition in the UK of owner-occupiers, a concept given a boost in the 1980s with the Thatcher idea of a "property owning democracy." Through long-term residence and inherited homes the UK has a generation of people in modest jobs with equally modest wages living in properties that it seems inconceivable they can afford. A situation where the annual rise in value of your home is way in excess of your annual salary is commonplace. Retiring Brits now look to trade-down to a smaller home, and look around the world for a second home.

The Dursleys fit the bill of a family with a modest income living in a home that has a price tag seemingly out of their reach. They have managed it because they bought years ago. Probably the bank account is empty and the car a wreck—their wealth is their house.

4. The Seven Potters

★★★★★

Assessment

Genius! Pretty much all the good guys are in this chapter, all acting with courage and dedication. The plot device of the seven Harry Potters is a bold and unexpected concept. This chapter works very well indeed.

Re-reading

If anything this chapter gets better. Re-reading allows us to sort out who was a protector and who a Harry Potter, who flew with whom, what happened to each on the journey. Rowling must have had it all planned out on paper. Additionally this chapter has much about it that is comic. The idea of producing six clone Harrys is like something out of a comic book or a B science fiction movie.

Heroes and Villains

Every one of the rescue party show bravery, even Mundungus, though his small store of courage deserts him. While the first chapter is the chapter of the villains, this is the chapter of heroes. The attackers are all playing roles. Voldemort's evil transcends the category of villain, while Snape's apparent malice is later found to be an accident.

The Secret Life of Severus Snape

Snape has of course betrayed the date of Harry's flight from Privet Drive to Voldemort—but he has withheld the crucial information that there will be seven Harry Potters. It is never properly established why he had to betray the date, rather than agree to the wrong date Yaxley gives. Had the date remained unknown to Voldemort it seems unlikely that there would have been so many Death Eaters guarding the area. Possibly we should assume that Voldemort is such a strong mind reader that it is not possible for Snape to conceal everything.

Snape's idea of the seven Potters is an unusual concept. When in a previous book Harry was moved by broomstick from Privet Drive to Grimmauld Place he had a substantial bodyguard, and the idea was to take a circuitous route to avoid detection, and that if there was an attack to fight to the death. Simple! The device of the seven Potters is far more subtle. Snape is aware that Voldemort wants to kill Harry personally and, the device ensures that there is an identification problem.

Snape's double agent status means that he has to play a realistic part in the subsequent fight. He does have to shoot curses at some of the escort party. Subsequently we learn that he shoots to miss; yet of course he does hit, taking off George's ear.

In the chase Snape follows the "Harry Potter" protected by Remus Lupin, and it seems he selects this pair to follow. Why this pair? The book doesn't tell us. In view of the dislike of Snape for Lupin in seems possible that he has selected this particular protector as part of his personal vendetta, but remember that he is shooting to miss. Rather it is possible that Snape thinks that Harry will be transported by Lupin. The view of most of the Death Eaters is that the most experienced person will protect Harry, therefore Mad Eye Moody, but Snape is well aware that Lupin has a special regard for Harry, and may have volunteered for the role. Snape is perhaps helping the most likely real Harry Potter get away by chasing this particular broomstick and shooting to miss. In support it may be noted that the curse he uses, *sectumsempra,* is one that he knows that Harry knows (Harry once ill-advisedly used it on Draco Malfoy) and for which Harry knows the counter-curse. By the choice of this vicious, deadly curse, Snape may even have in mind reminding Harry that he must be on guard both against the Dark Lord's ruthlessness and against the hot-tempered arrogance that James Potter sometimes exhibited as a young man.

The Gender Issue

The presentation of women and men in the Harry Potter novels can be explored through the fourteen characters of this chapter, seven "protectors" and seven "Harry Potters." To appear equal, it should be seven women and seven men, and the three or four of the protectors—the most valiant role—should be women and the same number men.

In fact the breakdown is as follows:

Protector	**"Harry Potter"**
Hagrid	Harry Potter
Mad-Eye Moody	Mundungus
Mr Weasley	Fred Weasley
Kingsley	Hermione
Tonks	Ron Weasley
Lupin	George Weasley
Bill	Fleur

Among the protectors all but one (Tonks) are male. Here as often in the Harry Potter novels the leadership roles are assigned to men.

Of the thirteen members of Harry's rescue party only three are women (Tonks, Hermione, Fleur)—while the fourteenth (Harry) is of course male.

The rescue is a quantifiable example of the apparent under-representation of women in roles of leadership and bravery. Presumably Rowling reflects society as it exists in the UK today; arguably she perpetuates and even promotes gender stereotypes.

Hagrid

The one person with whom Harry Potter should not travel is Hagrid. Hagrid is not a qualified wizard and cannot ride a broomstick. He is also rather accident-prone, and, while a sterling character and one of the most deeply loved people in Harry's life, would likely be outmatched by an accomplished Dark wizard in a straight-up battle. It is possible to speculate on the discussion that took place among the rescue party as to who should protect Harry, and perhaps conclude that the rescuers thought it was a bluff. Harry, a superb broomstick rider, will surely be on a broomstick protected by the most experienced wizard, Mad Eye Moody. It certainly makes sense to avoid this most obvious scenario, but putting Harry in a flying motorbike's sidecar protected by Hagrid seems foolish.

The scene links with much that has gone before in the Harry Potter novels. Sixteen years ago Hagrid used the same motorbike to take Harry from his dead parents' home. There is a parallel between Hagrid taking him into the security of Privet Drive after an attack by Voldemort and now Hagrid taking him out of that security, chased by Voldemort. There's also a parallel with the flying Ford Anglia which took Harry and Ron to Hogwarts in *Harry Potter and the Chamber of Secrets*—though the Anglia ride is mostly fun while the motorbike ride is horror from start to finish.

"Across Three Counties" is the one-phrase description of the chase of Harry from Privet Drive (in Surrey). It is revealing. To the east and south from Surrey the sea is reached by crossing just one county (Sussex or Kent). To the north is London, a city rather than a county. It seems that Harry and Hagrid traveled west. The route appears to be from Surrey across Hampshire and—assuming they are flying in a straight line—into Wiltshire. Thus the home of the Tonks family is in Wiltshire, the county of Stonehenge.

5. *Fallen Warrior*

Assessment

There's a mood change with this chapter. While the first chapter is horrific, the horror is Gothic, almost fantasy horror. The murder is of Charity Burbage, a Hogwarts teacher we readers don't know and cannot therefore have any affection for. By contrast the murder in this chapter is of Mad Eye Moody. Moody does not have the central role of some of the other deaths of the series—Sirius Black or Albus Dumbledore—but he is one of the good guys and a leading member of the Order of the Phoenix, and his death brings home the shock of Voldemort's attack. At least as shocking is the injury sustained by George Weasley (whose ear is cut off by Severus Snape) and the fear of the Weasley family. This chapter, more than those that have gone before, sets the brooding menace of the book.

Re-reading

This chapter is dominated by the serious. The surprise on re-reading is how much there is in it that is trivial or even comic. Hagrid knocking over an aspidistra and requiring medicinal brandy, George Weasley's joke on his own lost ear, Fleur's accented English—all these aspects have real humor. Rowling gives a true-life mix of events large and small, sad and comic, in a very full chapter.

Heroes and Villains

The title leaves no doubt that Mad-Eye Moody is the hero. While his actions have perhaps been no more brave than any other of the rescue party, he has paid with his life. George's injury pales in the face of the finality of death. Curiously Mundungus is not presented as a villain. While his cowardice appears to have caused Moody's death there is an implicit pulling back from blaming him or anyone else.

Logic

Lupin asserts that "the only people who could have told [Voldemort] were directly involved in the plan". Similarly Fleur believes that someone "let slip" the date. This is valid on its face,, and suggests that one of the thirteen in the rescue party must have betrayed Harry. As a consequence suspicion falls on Mundungus (the coward) and Hagrid, who in *Harry Potter and the Philosopher's Stone* had let slip important information. Yet Lupin's logic is wrong. In fact the leak is from the true author of the plan, Snape, who suggested the plan to Mundungus.

The Secret Life of Severus Snape

We are not told quite what the Death Eaters do after the rescue party (save Mad Eye Moody and Mundungus) reach their places of safety. Presumably they regroup. Voldemort quickly leaves, because just a short time later Harry senses that he is torturing Ollivander. It seems likely that all of the Death Eaters, therefore including Snape, search for the body of Mad Eye Moody, and as his magic eye was later used by Dolores Umbridge on her office door we can assume that they found him.

An Aspidistra is the pot plant in the Tonks's home. A strange choice from Rowling! It would be hard to buy one today in a British florist or nursery as they are out of fashion. Indeed the most likely place to encounter them is in George Orwell's novel *Keep the Aspidistra Flying* (1936) where they are seen as a symbol of middle class respectability. Here as so often in the Harry Potter series details of the magic world are in effect old fashioned British details. I doubt Rowling has an aspidistra on a delicate table in her home (as Andromeda Tonks does) but it is quite possible that her grandmother did.

Loss of an Ear is a curious injury. That it should be George's ear that is cut off by Snape's curse is strange indeed. We later discover that Snape was aiming to miss, so it is purely bad luck that has caused this particular accident. The menace and threat that runs through the chapter probably does require that in order for realism to be maintained there should be an injury of some sort to at least one character, but why this particular injury? The artist Vincent van Gogh famously cut off his own ear, but there seems no parallel with George.

6. The Ghoul in Pyjamas

★★★★

Assessment

This chapter offers a good, Rowling mix of entertainment—the humor of the ghost in pyjamas—along with some serious thought. Hermione's comments on the human soul go beyond her usual academic brilliance—indeed they are profound. And that's not what any of us expect from the average children's book or any book, and it reminds us that there is nothing average about the Harry Potter novels.

Re-reading

A second look at the chapter reveals an atmosphere of brooding fear. The reality of the situation is that three young adults plan to defeat the most powerful wizard of the age and know they face both their own deaths and perhaps the deaths of their families. Most at risk is the Weasley family. The situation cannot be avoided, but the dark plot-line does take the shine off the enjoyment of the chapter.

Heroes and Villains

Here as so often in this book it is the trio of Harry, Ron and Hermione who are the heroes. All three have made provision for their families realizing that their families will be in danger—and all three appear to have accepted the possibility of their own death.

The Secret Life of Severus Snape

Remorse is needed to put together a soul damaged by evil. It is Snape who has done evil and who has come to feel remorse. His penance is life-long. Everything he does is prompted by his remorse. He is not concerned about his reputation, instead willing to allow the world to believe him a murderer; his concern is only to do the right thing.

There is an implied contrast with Voldemort. Snape's redemption starts around the time when Voldemort kills Lily and James Potter, a tragedy that makes him aware that he has been wrong. Voldemort has the experience of almost dying with the power-base he has created destroyed. He could use this experience as the beginnings of remorse. The spectral Voldemort has the time for remorse and to heal his soul. Instead he chooses the path of evil.

The Soul

Hermione offers readers a succinct description of the soul. She points out that if right now she killed Ron she would do no damage to his soul. Ron needs the message spelt out. In Hermione's words "whatever happens to your body, your soul will survive, untouched."

Hermione sums up a lot of Christian theology in a few words. Right at the start of the Bible we are told that "man became a living soul" (*Genesis* 2:7), though the whole of the Old Testament actually says very little about the soul or what happens to it after death.

Rather the idea of the soul surviving after the death of the body is something which comes from Christ's promise of eternal life in the Gospels. Various Christian churches have come up with all sorts of different ideas as to just what the soul might be and what happens to it. The Roman Catholic tradition sees souls sleeping until the end of the world, and then all souls being judged at the same time. The Protestant tradition sees souls as being judged immediately after death. The Harry Potter novels seem to suggest this Protestant view—which makes sense as Rowling is a Protestant.

In the *Preface* Rowling quotes William Penn's *More Fruits of Solitude*. Two lines above the section she quotes is the line "Death cannot kill what never dies." Death cannot kill the undying soul. Hermione is in full agreement with William Penn.

Pyjamas are rather dated in Britain. There are times when it is clear that Rowling has a sense of humor, and this is one of them. Pyjamas—pajamas in the US spelling—were an import from Britain's Indian Empire, but they've developed in Britain. In Britain the term refers to a two-piece suit of nightwear worn by boys—often called jim-jams or 'jamers. It is vaguely amusing that seventeen-year-old Ron is wearing them. Today in UK shops, adult sizes seem intended mostly for men who expect a stay in hospital, though a generation ago they would have been usual nightwear for all. As so often in the Harry Potter novels the magic world described is old fashioned Britain, the world in which Rowling grew up.

7. The Will of Albus Dumbledore

★★★★

Assessment

Dumbledore continues to direct the lives of Harry and friends even after his death. The bequests are of course significant, something the reader instantly realizes even though we cannot make out the significance.

Re-Reading

The material bequests in his will are just a small part of his legacy. His reputation is another part of his legacy, both the Dumbledore of Doge and the Dumbledore of Skeeter. Through the book we come to see another sort of legacy, that of the impact on people and particularly on following generations. Harry has a choice between Dumbledore's advice—to seek out the horcruxes—and the alternative of seeking the hallows. Eventually, Harry follows Dumbledore, and it is this that is perhaps the most important legacy that Dumbledore leaves.

Heroes and Villains

The Weasley family are going out of their way to welcome new members. The forthcoming wedding, hosted by the Weasleys, welcomes Fleur as their daughter-in-law and the Delacour family as their extended family. However trying the women of the family may find Fleur she has been accepted as part of their family ever since her stirring speech at Bill's bedside at the end of *Harry Potter and the Half-Blood Prince.* Equally welcoming is the their decision to treat Harry as if a son by giving him a coming-of-age watch. They behave in an exemplary fashion.

Rufus Scrimgeour's behavior deserves censure. He abuses his position in an effort to intimidate, resulting ultimately to violence in the form of the wand-burn to Harry's T-shirt.

The Will

Harry, Ron and Hermione seem to think it strange that a whole month has passed since Dumbledore's death before they are presented with the bequests he has left them. In most jurisdictions, certainly including England, the legal process of proving a will and giving bequests takes a lot longer than a month, even when wills are simple. Of course in the fictitious world that is Harry Potter, Rowling can establish any convention she likes, but it is unusual to see her depart from the norms of British society. A possible solution is within the concept of Scots law. The United Kingdom does not have a unified legal system, but rather the kingdoms that form it have their own independent systems, and Scots law is fundamentally different from English law. Dumbledore lived and died in Scotland (the assumed location of Hogwarts) and it does seem likely that his affairs would be dealt with under Scots law. The key concept is the Scots *testament testamentar*, which deals with bequests other than land and property, and is usually enacted very quickly, sometimes at the time of the funeral.

The Secret Life of Severus Snape

Dumbledore has left Snape the task of helping Harry, which includes ensuring that he gets the real Sword of Gryffindor, though Dumbledore has not told Snape why Harry needs it. Presumably Dumbledore is worried that Voldemort may one day read Snape's mind and so discover that Dumbledore knew about his horcruxes. It appears to be Snape who has the sword copied and puts the fake in the headmaster's office at Hogwarts—the real one is presumably concealed in his rooms at the school.

Scrimgeour

Of course Scrimgeour does not behave well in this encounter. He is indeed the villain of the chapter. Yet let us just for a moment try to see it his way. Harry is "the boy that lived." Scrimgeour probably doesn't himself believe Harry is the key player who will defeat Voldemort, but he is politically astute and does believe that Harry has enormous value to his government. And Scrimgeour really is trying to defeat Voldemort, however much of a mess he is making of doing this. Yet Harry has previously refused to lend him his support, much as Dumbledore had previously done. And, horror of horrors, Dumbledore seems to have passed some message to Harry and friends through his strange bequests. Readers can imagine the ingenuity that has gone into trying to work out what these bequests might mean, and it is seemingly a decision born of desperation that Scrimgeour will himself present the bequests. He must be very disappointed that he learns nothing.

Scrimgeour appears in this chapter as if an enemy of Harry. Yet ultimately he dies trying to save Harry.

"I open at the close"

What a superb riddle! The meaning is not obvious—until you know what it means, when it suddenly becomes obvious. The close is of course the close of life. The snitch opens when Harry is about to die.

8. The Wedding

Assessment

This is a chapter in the style of a thousand and one weddings in literature and film where the happy couple's big day is interrupted by an event. Here the marriage takes place as planned but the reception is rather spoilt by the arrival of the Death Eaters. That something untoward will happen is curiously predictable! The fact that the wedding occurs in the early parts of the book, rather than at the end, is a clue for the experienced reader.

Re-Reading

Very little of this chapter is actually about the wedding. I'm willing to guess that most readers of the book would have to think twice to come up with the full names of bride and groom (Fleur Isabelle Delacour and William Arthur Weasley), and only a very few lines are given to the ceremony itself. We don't actually see much of bride or groom; we do instead see some strange relatives and friends of the bride and groom brought together by the big day. Surely every family has its Auntie Muriel! And what family gathering would be complete without an eccentric Xenophilus Lovegood to embarrass everyone! Rowling presents a believable feel of a big wedding.

Amateurs

The Order of the Phoenix are clearly a lot of bungling amateurs with very little sense. The wedding brings together all leading members of the Order. There is no possibility that secrecy can be preserved with so many people involved. The reality is that Voldemort must have known that most of his enemies would be in one location at a specified time. And he could imagine that within the context of a party some might be unprepared to fight, or even drunk from too much wedding drinking. He can guess too that Harry may well be there.

The safeguard is the enchantments around The Burrow. Now clearly they are effective, but only so long as the Ministry of Magic remains. In effect the wedding gives Voldemort a deadline to bring about the fall of the Ministry, and it is reasonable to imagine that he puts all possible energy into just this.

Heroes and Villains

A wedding is the day for the happy couple. Though the reader sees very little of Bill and Fleur they have to be heroes. The guests don't really behave themselves—but do wedding guests ever? Auntie Muriel is presented as a spiteful woman who uses her age to excuse her nastiness, though she is hardly a villain.

The Secret Life of Severus Snape

Voldemort and the Death Eaters know about the wedding, so presumably Snape does also, There is no evidence that he either helps Harry or hinders the Death Eaters, presumably because he has opportunity to do neither.

Ginevra is revealed as the full form of Ginny Weasley's name. Readers who have speculated might have assumed Virginia. The real-life Ginevra that Rowling might have come across is Ginevra de'Benci, the red-haired sixteen-year old beauty of a Leonardo da Vinci painting, now in the "National Gallery of Art" in Washing-ton. Ginevra de'Benci is therefore the same age as Ginny in *Harry Potter and the Deathly Hallows* and like Ginny has red hair.

For readers familiar with Roman mythology, the name Ginevra is somewhat reminiscent of Minerva, the goddess of wisdom, a trait which Ginny is clearly portrayed as possessing.

Pascal's Wager is Doge's solution to whether Harry should or should not believe in the merits of Dumbledore. According to Doge, Harry should chose what to believe.

The prime philosophical statement of choice in belief is Pascal's Wager. The French philosopher Blaise Pascal states that there is no objective proof for the existence (or non-existence) of God, but also that it is infinitely better to believe. If God doesn't exist whether you believe or don't believe in God makes no difference to your fate after death. But if God does exist only those who believe will have an eternity in paradise, while the fate of non-believers is variously perceived as annihilation or an eternity of torment in hell. We should therefore choose to believe in God. The reward to believers is infinitely great. The loss to non-believers is nothing. Therefore take the wager that God exists.

Pascal assumes that belief is a matter of choice. The idea is not that a person should pretend belief, but rather that they should really believe. He also regarded God within the Christian tradition, disregarding the view of some Christian groups and some other religions that only those who worship God precisely as they do can go to heaven. For Pascal the idea is that if a person lives their life within a Christian context open to belief they will indeed believe, and that belief will be real and unfeigned. We can choose what we believe. This is precisely what Doge urges Harry to do as far as Dumbledore is concerned. In less eloquent terms Hermione says the same.

The Swastika has undergone the sort of change of meaning that is attributed to the changing referents of the "sign of the deathly hallows." It crops up in very many ancient cultures, but in Europe is best known from Ancient Greek decoration, where it is called the *gammadion* or *Greek key*. It is primarily decorative, though those associations which exist for it do seem to be positive. In 1920 the Nazi party adopted this symbol as their own. The taint the symbol now has is comparable with that Viktor Krum perceives as associated with the sign of the deathly hallows.

9. A Place to Hide

Assessment

And they're off! Up to this point Harry has been in the care of the wizarding world. The Order of the Phoenix have moved him safely from Privet Drive, while the Weasley family have become his adopted home. As Harry, Ron and Hermione leave the wedding they leave this security. Ron could go back—indeed when later he walks out this is more or less what he does. Hermione could hide in the muggle world, perhaps with her parents in Australia. However for Harry there is no way back.

Re-Reading

In the terms of the magic world Harry and friends are adults because they are over 17. Most nations—including the "muggle" world in the UK—see 18 as the age of adulthood. If they are adults they are very young adults. They are not comfortable in the adult world of Tottenham Court Road (which is not the nicest street in London, but not particularly threatening either) and they are uneasy with the adult task of ordering a coffee in a cafe. They are immediately challenged by being attacked by two Death Eaters, and while the invisibility cloak tips the odds in their favor their abilities are well demonstrated. Then they face an adult choice—to kill or not to kill. A lot is being asked of these 17-year olds.

Heroes and Villains

Hermione saves all three. It is Hermione who has packed the belongings they will need, including the invisibility cloak, Hermione who transports them to the safety of Tottenham Court Road. The sort of hard work and careful preparation that in previous books she has put into her Hogwarts exams has gone into her preparations for departure from the Weasleys' home. The chapter has clear villains in the two Death Eaters. Their intention is the murder of three seventeen-year olds. There is no pretense at questioning Harry for the murder of Dumbledore or any hint of a justification for their actions. Rather Harry is perceived as a threat by Voldemort and a focus for opposition, and Ron and Hermione are simply bonuses.

The Secret Life of Severus Snape

In the days following Dumbledore's death the Order of the Phoenix vacates their headquarters of Grimmauld Place because they believe that Snape will betray the premises to Voldemort. The plot device is that prior to Dumbledore's death only Dumbledore was the "secret keeper" who could introduce people to the building; after Dumbledore's death everyone who had access became a secret keeper.

Had Snape intended to betray the headquarters to Voldemort he could have done it within minutes of Dumbledore's death. It isn't clear just when safety devices were put up to restrict Snape's ability to betray the headquarters, but it certainly wasn't in a few minutes. Voldemort would of course have demanded that Snape should betray the headquarters—if he knew Snape was a member of the Order of the Phoenix. The most plausible submerged plot is that Voldemort did not ever know that Snape was a member.

Sometime in the month or so after the death of Dumbledore, Snape has visited the former headquarters of Grimmauld Place. As Voldemort did not know that Snape was—and in his heart still is—a member of the Order of the Phoenix, he does not know that Snape has access, and presumably Snape doesn't tell him. The "body bind curse" that has been placed on the building to stop Snape revealing its presence to Voldemort is not actually needed.

Quite why Snape visits Grimmauld Place is not fully explained. He takes away part of a letter from his childhood sweetheart Lily Evans, Harry's mum.

Tottenham Court Road is a curious place to visit. Why Hermione thinks of Tottenham Court Road is not revealed—indeed when asked she glosses over the question. The road is the northward continuation of Charing Cross Road above the intersection with Oxford Street, but it lacks the respectability of these two major shopping streets. The road is decidedly seedy—it is where betting shops and sex shops share space with mainstream shops and offices. It is surprising that Hermione has ever been there. Perhaps the seedy atmosphere and potential for crime is what Rowling wishes to evoke by choosing this location.

Ron says that Tottenham Court Road is close to the Leaky Cauldron in Charing Cross Road. The surprise is that Ron knows London this well. True his father works in London, but at every opportunity through the Harry Potter novels Ron displays his near-total ignorance of the muggle world.

Building Societies are curiously British. Hermione has a building society account. This is a British invention—a type of bank which as its core business offers savings accounts, using these savings to fund mortgages specifically for people to buy the home they live in. Building Societies are mutuals, owned by the people who save with them. Once it was easier to get a mortgage to buy a house from a Building Society with which you were a long-term saver, so parents would open savings accounts for their children and encourage them to save with the intention that one day they would become a home owner. Here as so often in this book Rowling is presenting a muggle world which reflects Britain in the 1970s and 1980s.

10. Kreacher's Tale

Assessment

There is a tale within a tale. Indeed in this chapter there are two. First we read a letter written by Harry Potter's mum, Lily, which gives a glimpse of the life the family led before Voldemort murdered Lily and James. Then Kreacher's tale explains why the locket recovered in Harry Potter and the Half Blood Prince is not in fact a horcrux, and where the real horcrux is now. These are two separate digressions, yet Rowling manages to integrate them into the story in a way that is smooth and compelling. This chapter works well.

Re-Reading

Earlier in the Harry Potter story, Kreacher played a key role in the murder of Sirius Black. While readers might feel that his role in the death was indirect (though Harry doesn't) he certainly broke the wing of a Hippogriff as his personal contribution to the plot. Kreacher is not a nice character. Yet in this chapter we come to sympathize with him. The abuse to which Voldemort subjected him was extreme. Sirius Black treats him with a contempt which he does not deserve. The Kreacher we see in this chapter is emotionally damaged. His loyalty is to previous generations of the Black family (particularly to Regulus) but also to other pure-blood wizards, many of whom seem to have treated him well.

Heroes and Villains

The tale told by Kreacher makes him the surprise hero of this chapter. He has a measure of responsibility for the murder of Sirius Black and is rude to Harry and friends, yet the pathos of his tale makes readers understand that he has in his time acted a heroic role. Perhaps if we truly understand people we can come to terms with their actions. By contrast Mundungus is revealed as a thief who steals from his friends. Readers have been inclined to believe with Harry that he did not betray the rescue party to Voldemort (and readers are right in this), and have been willing to forgive him his cowardice which contributed to Moody's death, but the simple crime of theft places him in the category of villain.

The Secret Life of Severus Snape

We are told that Snape visits Grimmauld Place. Presumably he is responsible for the mess caused by searching it. Nowhere is it made clear why he visits and why he searches, or why his search creates so much mess. All that appears to be taken is part of a letter to Sirius Black written by Lily Potter. Was Snape merely searching for mementos of Lily?

Snape knows about the portrait which provides a window from the headmaster's study at Hogwarts into Grimmauld Place. He must know that Harry and friends are there almost as soon as they arrive.

It is not clear why Snape does not pass the Sword of Gryffindor to Harry while he is at Grimmauld Place. It cannot be that the curses that Mad Eye Moody has put on the building are too strong for him to enter as he's already been there. Perhaps he feels he cannot do so now Harry and friends are there without betraying his double agent role. Additionally the need for the Sword to pass to Harry in a manner which is perilous is hard to contrive within the safe environment of Grimmauld Place. In short there are good reasons why Snape does not at this time pass the sword to Harry, yet his failure to do so delays by some months the destruction of the Horcrux.

11. The Bribe

Assessment

This chapter is unsettling, and isn't the nicest read. The action takes place while Kreacher is tracking down Mundungus and has at its heart the encounter with Remus Lupin. This meeting should be a happy moment. Readers of the Harry Potter novels will know Lupin as the teacher who went the extra mile to support Harry and the friend of Harry's father James and of Sirius Black. He comes with an offer of help. Yet within a few minutes Lupin and Harry have a serious argument. Perhaps the best that can be said is that neither behave well. Harry's comments are too confrontational (perhaps a reminder that he is just seventeen) while Lupin seems unwilling to treat Harry as an adult and give his comments a serious answer. Perhaps the problem is that age seventeen isn't quite a child and isn't quite an adult.

Re-Reading

There's a plot hole of sorts in this chapter. Voldemort knows—or at least could know—all the information that Lupin uses to prove his identity to Harry. At best the facts serve as a basic check that Lupin is indeed Lupin, but it is hit and miss. The exchange underlines just how amateurish the Order of the Phoenix is.

Lupin's visit is also misguided because it is dangerous, and in the way he does it, it is needlessly dangerous. If Snape had betrayed the location to Voldemort then it is likely that one or more Death Eaters would be present. It is surprising that Lupin doesn't visit with someone to support him. Perhaps we are to infer that the Order of the Phoenix is too badly damaged. Or perhaps it underlines that the visit is Lupin's own idea in the hope of finding himself a task which would take him away from his wife.

Heroes and Villains

Both Harry and Lupin behave badly in this chapter. Both behave in a way which is easy to understand, but that doesn't make it right. For that matter Ron and Hermione fail to offer a solution. This chapter shows us that the good guys can get it wrong.

A Plot Hole?

Harry says to Lupin that he cannot reveal the task that Dumbledore has set him. But why not?

Presumably we are to infer that Dumbledore thought that the most effective way of destroying horcruxes was to ensure that Voldemort didn't know they were looking for them. He has himself destroyed Marvolo's ring and confirmed that Voldemort cannot sense their destruction, so in theory it would be possible to destroy every one of them without Voldemort knowing, and this was the trump card those fighting him had. Clearly the knowledge of the horcruxes should be a secret, yet entrusting it just to Harry (and to

Ron and Hermione) seems strange. If all three were killed or captured, or if they simply decided not to act, then the key knowledge Dumbledore had obtained would be useless. Additionally support from members of the Order of the Phoenix would help find the horcruxes.

Rowling asks us to believe that Dumbledore trusted Harry more than the Order of the Phoenix. Later we learn that Dumbledore wanted to slow Harry down, so perhaps not giving him too much help is part of this scheme. Yet Harry's refusal to trust Lupin seems surprising.

Lupin

That Lupin leaves Grimmauld Place in a rage is no surprise. The surprise is that he doesn't go back later. In earlier books Snape has expressed doubts about the character of Lupin, and his teenage years as part of the Marauders gang at Hogwarts shows a reckless side to his nature. Readers have tended to see Lupin as Harry's mentor and friend and supported him, but this chapter reminds us that he is flawed. Perhaps it reminds us that we are all flawed.

The Secret Life of Severus Snape

"No sign of Severus then?" Lupin's question is pertinent—Snape had access to Grimmauld Place and should be using that access.

If he were working for Voldemort he should be using his access to help Voldemort. Even if he couldn't bring in other Death Eaters he should be sifting through the hastily-vacated headquarters of the Order of the Phoenix for anything they might have left behind. He might certainly interrogate Kreacher. Rowling raises in passing the surprise that he is not there but doesn't allow her characters to become aware of just how significant this is.

But of course Snape is not working for Voldemort. He should be able to guess that Harry and friends may well be there, as he knows they have access and have stayed there before, but he isn't going to walk in as Lupin did because it would blow his cover.

Mould-on-the-Wold should exist! Garton-on-the-Wolds, Middleton-on-the-Wolds, Holme-on-the-Wolds, Wold Newton, Mouldsworth—all these are English place names. But not Mould-on-the-Wold! It's one of those names which doesn't exist but probably should, and probably should have a cheese named after it! Maybe sooner or later some dweller in the Yorkshire Wolds will think Mould-on-the-Wold a great name to give to their home as a tribute to the Harry Potter novels.

"Bleedin' 'eroes" is Cockney. Mundungus Fletcher's language indicates that he is a Cockney from London's East End speaking the unique dialect of the market traders. Rowling transcribes his accent with initial "h" lost throughout: "'unted down by 'ouse-elves." She does not treat readers to a great deal more of this rhyming dialect which was a slang developed specifically to exclude outsiders, so people who were not Cockneys would not understand what was being said. Mundungus is in quite a two-and-eight (state) that Harry didn't get on the dog (dog-and-bone, telephone, make a phone call) to contact him but instead sent an 'ouse-elf to nab (apprehend) him.

12. Magic is Might

★★★★★

Assessment

This is an action-packed chapter. Great fun, and a truly satisfying read.

Re-Reading

Harry and friends have become proactive. The flight from Privet Drive is made necessary by Voldemort's threat to Harry; the flight from the wedding at the Weasleys' home is made necessary by the attack by the Death Eaters; the events in Tottenham Court Road are again part of the flight. Here the pace changes—Harry is attacking Voldemort. By seeking and destroying the horcruxes he is destroyed Voldemort, piece by piece.

Heroes and Villains

Harry and friends are the heroes of this tale of daring. Within the Ministry they encounter people good and bad, a moral spectrum from the thorough decency of Ron's Dad to the love of torture of Umbridge. Yet in a sense all in the Ministry are villains as all have gone along wit the system. They haven't resigned or made a stand, but continued to do their job and take a pay-check from the government controlled by Voldemort.

Might is Right or Survival of the Fittest is the title of Ragnar Redbeard's 1890 book, a book title which appears to be echoed in the title of this chapter. Taking as its starting point the Darwinian evolutionary mechanism of "survival of the fittest," Redbeard seeks to advance a version of Social Darwinism which states that morality derives from power and should have no regard for the weak. Redbeard specifically rejects the moral code of the Old Testament which he sees as a false philosophy derived from what he terms "weepful" messiahs. For Redbeard the only source of moral right is the exercise of power, the "club", the "gallows" and the "sword." In his conclusion he addresses "Christ-deluded imbeciles", criticizing "moonstruck meeklings" and "bleeding lambs" and offering instead "molten hell."

The political legacy is that this repugnant book influenced fascist and racist beliefs, specifically including those of the Nazi party. There is also a religious legacy in that Satanists have seen the book as embodying a Satanic view of nature. Today the book is (thankfully) little read, though its title is remembered as a "justification" of oppression.

In this chapter we see a Ministry of Magic which is enforcing a racist doctrine (expressed as "pure-blood" wizards and witches) and terrorizing the weak with "dementors." This is indeed the world of "might is right," and a clear presentation of the odious doctrine that all the Harry Potter novels oppose. This is what

Harry and friends are fighting against, and this is what ultimately Harry defeats. The lesson of the series is that might is not right.

13. The Muggle-born Registration Commission

★★★★

Assessment

Horrific stuff! Umbridge has shown her faults earlier in the series with her willingness to torture children, yet seeing her evil approved by a powerful system—the Ministry—is that much more frightening. This is the spirit of the Third Reich. Umbridge is revealed as a torturer, carrying on her role while those around do nothing.

Re-Reading

A key concept that flows from this chapter is the structure for the whole book. Seemingly this chapter can be seen as the start of a second section to the book. All the structure the reader sees is the thirty-six chapters. Yet there is a perceptible three-part structure to the novel:

- Chapters 1-12. The flight of Harry, through to the start of the first mission to eliminate horcruxes. In all the previous novels the introductory section is shorter and ends with the journey to Hogwarts, but in this final novel Harry and friends of course do not go to Hogwarts.

- Chapters 13-24. The school year. In all the other books this is spent at Hogwarts, but in this final book it is spent under canvas.
- Chapters 25-36. The decision to seek horcruxes not hallows, and the return to Hogwarts for the Battle of Hogwarts.

It seems likely that Rowling planned the novel as three sets of twelve chapters.

Heroes and Villains

As in the previous chapter Harry and friends are heroes while many at the Ministry are villains. The chapter lets us see the Cattermoles as a couple traumatized by Voldemort's regime. While Mrs Cattermole is the victim of the "muggle-born registration committee" her husband Reg Cattermole works in the Ministry which houses that committee.

Registration

The concept of registration of a people seen by a nation as undesirable is not an invention of Rowling. During the 1930s and the years of the Second World War registration of Jewish people was a part of the Nazi system. For example in the Greek city of Thessaloniki, the city's occupation by Germany in April 1941 was followed first by registration of the large Jewish community The registration was a tool that permitted the subsequent extermination of that population, with the result that barely a thousand were still alive when the city was liberated in October 1944. Throughout Nazi Europe registration was a prelude to extermination.

The world readers glimpse in the Ministry of Magic resembles the world of Nazi Germany.

14. The Thief

Here's a challenge for avid Harry Potter readers—who is the thief named in the chapter heading and what does he steal? In fact we don't learn his name in this chapter (it is in fact Grindelwald)—rather he's simply the young man who steals the unbeatable wand from Gregorovitch. Readers do need this plot information, but not now, and as readers don't at this stage know about the deathly hallows there isn't a mental box to put it in.

Re-Reading

Perhaps a change of pace is needed after the frantic action of the past two chapters. Readers need a break. But its not clear that readers are particularly interested in Ron's injuries, or at this stage in the action in what events linked to Gregorovitch. A truly critical assessment would condense this chapter to a few paragraphs added in to the chapter before or after, or perhaps somewhere else in the book. For readers who feel the middle section of the novel is slow, this chapter is a key example.

Heroes and Villains

My personal response to this chapter is that I cannot engage with it to the extent of feeling that anyone is particularly good or bad. Just as I'm not engaged with the characters I'm not engaged with this chapter. Do we need it? It certainly gets the shortest *Re-Reading* write up of any chapter in this book.

The Secret Life of Severus Snape

Once Yaxley enters Grimmauld Place he will summon other Death Eaters, perhaps including Snape. It seems clear that a Death Eater as senior as Snape, even if not summoned, will soon learn of the fall of Grimmauld Place. He knows that Harry and friends have been there, and now he knows that they have fled.

Essence of Dittany seems to be an invention of Rowling, but the plant dittany certainly exists and with healing properties. It is a rare herb found in remote mountain areas of Crete, typically growing on cliffs within gorges. Hippocrates, the Greek "father of medicine", describes dittany as a medicinal herb which is particularly useful for healing wounds. In Virgil's *Aeneid* (book 12), Venus heals the warrior Aeneas with dittany from Crete. The herb has also been credited with aphrodisiac properties. Far more common than dittany from Crete is false dittany, also called white dittany and burning bush. This is a common Mediterranean herb —completely unlike the true dittany of Crete—which secretes an oil which has a lemon smell and which does have some healing properties.

It is not clear whether Hermione's essence of dittany is made from Cretan dittany or false dittany. However it is very likely that Rowling has read the *Aeneid* and will have come across the herb there.

15. The Goblin's Revenge

Assessment

Once again Rowling uses the device of a story within the story, this time the overheard conversation of Griphook and his companions. The coincidence is enormous. The chance of Harry and friends encountering somewhere in the wilds of Britain people they know is minuscule. That these friends should be saying something important at the time when they are overheard is an even bigger coincidence. It is an easy way to present readers with information and reads well, but it does require from the reader a willingness to overlook the plot device of an impossible coincidence.

Re-Reading

Events lead up to Ron's departure, and this is where the reader's focus should be. The chapter is one of many which raises ethical issues, here around Ron's behavior. It makes the reader think.

Heroes and Villains

Ron is the villain of this chapter. He acts badly. Later we find that he realizes this almost immediately after walking out of Harry and Hermione. The contrast is with Hermione who sets aside her personal feelings for Ron to do what is right. She isn't happy about this, but she is the unsung hero.

Ron's Departure

Harry, Ron and Hermione have not always seen eye to eye. In the very first novel Harry and Ron at first don't like Hermione, and it is only after they rescue her from a troll that they become friends. There is a major falling-our between Harry and Ron in *Harry Potter and the Goblet of Fire*, where Ron is jealous of the attention Harry receives. There's also been a falling out between Hermione and Ron when Ron becomes infatuated with Lavender Brown. So yes there have been squabbles.

But now they are adults (at least in the terms of the magic world of Harry Potter, where age seventeen is adult). Perhaps we might expect better. In fairness to Ron he has had an horrific experience at the Ministry of Magic, has received disturbing news about his family, has had weeks of hunger and cold, and has recently been injured, and additionally appears adversely affected by proximity with Voldemort's locket. Walking out should not in itself be censured.

Where we might wish to censure him is that he seeks to encourage Hermione to leave with him. That scenario would leave Harry on his own, and it is very hard to see how he could continue with the quest unaided. Perhaps he would seek out members of the Order of the Phoenix; probably they would see hiding him as the best option. These maybes aren't explored in the book, yet the reality is that Ron comes close to derailing the only way of stopping Voldemort.

The Secret Life of Severus Snape

In this chapter we get a glimpse of Snape's activities as headmaster of Hogwarts. His punishment of Ginny and friends for entering his study and attempting to steal the sword of Gryffindor is described as harsh, yet the reality is that it is lenient. Asking them to help Hagrid with a task in the Forbidden Forest is a type of punishment that Harry and Ron have endured in the very first book (*Harry Potter and the Philosopher's Stone / Sorcerer's Stone*) and is perhaps best regarded as character forming.

As a consequence of the attempted theft, Snape moves what he must know is the fake sword of Gryffindor from Hogwarts to Gringotts. Why?

Presumably there are a couple of reasons why keeping the sword at Hogwarts has become problematic. If Ginny and friends should manage to steal it and should manage to get it to Harry—two very big ifs—then Harry would have a dud sword that would not act as required. Snape knows that if Ginny and friends had succeeded they may actually have hampered Harry. But Snape must also be aware that the attention of the Death Eaters might be drawn to the sword by the attempted theft, particularly that the Carrows who are teaching at Hogwarts might become interested in it. It may well occur to one of them to wonder just why it was left to Harry, and perhaps therefore to examine it, and perhaps the fact that it is a fake would have been discovered. Putting the sword in the bank does seem a solution. Snape must be aware that goblins would recognize that it is a fake, but presumably guesses their professional code will stop them mentioning it. If they did report the information it would presumably be just to Snape as headmaster of Hogwarts.

16. Godric's Hollow

Assessment

Readers are likely to miss Ron. Yes there have been adventures in past books which involve just two of the three (usually Harry and Ron), but it is nonetheless a departure from the usual "three musketeers" format. Visits to the house where Harry's parents died and to the graveyard are not comfortable. This is not a fun chapter.

Re-Reading

This chapter encourages the reader to think about family deaths. In the graveyard we see the graves of Harry Potter's parents, of Dumbledore's family and some ancient graves. The implied reminder is that death is inevitable. The Potters' family home, preserved in the state following Voldemort's attack, has become a sort of shrine to Harry as "the boy who lived."

Heroes and Villains

The chapter is retrospective in its coverage. Readers see the house where Harry's parents were murdered, and the heroic actions of Harry's parents are stressed. There is heroism of a sort in the people who visit the Potter home and leave a message of support.

The Secret Life of Severus Snape

We are told that Phineas Nigellus, the old Hogwarts' headmaster in the portrait, "venerated Snape.".To Harry and to the readers this veneration seem like an error of judgment—after all we think we know that Snape is a murderer and a Death Eater. The explanation for the veneration is that Nigellus, like Snape, was a member of Slytherin House, though this alone is hardly an adequate reason. Rather it seems that Nigellus has perceived the true worth of Snape, something that Harry and the readers fail to see until the final chapters. I'm not sure that any person should be venerated, but Snape certainly warrants our respect and our admiration. And curmudgeonly old Nigellus has got it right!

English Churchyards are part of the fabric of the English landscape, and Godric's Hollow is within the mold of thousands of English village—a cluster of houses around an old church and churchyard. As a rule of thumb the ground level of an English churchyard rises by a foot every century, with the result that many churchyards are several feet higher than the surrounding land—and often now higher than the floor of the church. In traditional English villages people live around their church and their dead.

17. Bathilda's Secret

Assessment

No first time reader would ever predict the key plot element of this chapter, the hiding place of Voldemort's snake, Nagini. As a part of a thriller this chapter scores top marks. Arguably the level of horror is so extreme that it rather takes the shine off the chapter. This is grotesque. Where did Rowling get the idea from?

Re-Reading

If in the previous chapter readers have found it strange to see Harry and Hermione on an adventure without Ron, here the implied question is whether events would have unfolded differently with Ron present. Would outspoken Ron have been as polite towards Nagini-Bathilda as was Hermione and allowed Harry to be parted from his friends? When the attack came would Ron's aid have allowed them to escape without Harry's wand being broken? The questions go well outside the book, yet Ron and Hermione have both made a commitment to support Harry and both should be present.

Heroes and Villains

Harry and Hermione are of course the heroes. Bathilda is another of Voldemort's victims but with a grotesque mutilation of her mortal remains. We don't know if her death was in any way heroic or simply sad. The chapter doesn't really have a villain, though perhaps there is an implicit condemnation of a society which has no care for an old lady who has lived all her life in the community. It seems that no-one knew she needed some help, and no-one noted her transformation.

The Secret Life of Severus Snape

There is nothing to indicate that Snape knew of the trap set at Godric's Hollow. Even had he known it is hard to see how he could have found a way to warn Harry or to neutralize the trap—though it is certain he would have wanted to.

Date and Time

Rowling goes out of her way to stress that Harry and Hermione had lost track of the date because they had not seen a newspaper for weeks, and didn't know that their arrival in Godric's Hollow was on Christmas Eve. I'm not sure how credible this is. Are we really to believe that the organized Hermione who in previous books has come up with revision schedules for herself, Harry and Ron would in this book have no idea of the date? Rather it seems to be a mechanism to get Harry and Hermione to Godric's Hollow on Christmas Eve.

They also visit in the late evening, surely a strange time to pay an unannounced visit on the elderly Bathilda. Their visit to the churchyard is therefore carried out by night, and without the benefit of light from their wands. We are told that there was light shining through the church windows, but the idea that this was enough to read gravestones seems implausible. The time of day lacks verisimilitude.

Indeed the point of the date and time seems to be that they are ultimately meeting with Bathilda just before midnight and are with her as Christmas Day comes in, with all the religious and cultural significance this day has.

Rowling sets up a contrast between the coming of Christ and the arrival of Voldemort. The people in Godric's Hollow know of the approach of Christmas Day; Harry knows Voldemort is coming. Christmas Day is greeted with the joyful peal of church bells; the coming of Voldemort is greeted with screams and the revelation of the horrible, dark magic where the snake Nagini inhabits the body of the dead Bathilda. Implicitly Rowling is making a religious statement. Perhaps readers should feel that Voldemort's splitting of his soul through the making of the horcruxes has transcended ordinary human sin and made him a devil. The timing presents Voldemort as an anti-Christ.

18. The Life and Lies of Albus Dumbledore

★★

Assessment

Fictional characters are created by an author but take on a life of their own. The novels, the films, the Harry Potter spin-offs, the popular acclamation, all means that by the time readers reach the final Harry Potter book the character of Dumbledore has become part of the common cultural milieu. Not even the creator of Dumbledore can tamper with the image of Dumbledore without censure from readers! This chapter discredits Dumbledore. The reader knows it is the view of a most unpleasant journalist, but also that there is some truth in what she says—and readers don't want to hear the truth about one of our favorite characters. Rather Dumbledore's memory should be treasured. Rowling is in this chapter speaking ill of the dead.

Re-Reading

Much of the worth of this chapter comes from linguistic subtleties, both in Skeeter's book and in the charged conversation between Harry and Hermione.

The language of Skeeter's book is masterly. Rowling, through Skeeter, manages to convey a view of Dumbledore which is at odds with the Dumbledore the reader knows. One technique she uses is to criticize not Dumbledore but those who associate with him, leading to a form of character assassination by association. Thus his friend Elphias Doge is given the nickname "Dogbreath" (unsourced, and for all we know invented by Skeeter) and described as "dim-witted." Bathilda is described as "nutty" (a sourced quote, though who Enid Smeek might be is not explained). The implication is that she suffers from senility, yet Skeeter manages to use this affliction to suggest that many years before she could not form a reasonable judgment about the Dumbledore family. In Skeeter's insinuating prose we see the hand of a master writer, the hand of course that of Rowling.

Heroes and Villains

The chapter reminds readers that Skeeter is nasty, something we first learn in *Harry Potter and the Goblet of Fire*. Through her jaded eyes we see the faults in Dumbledore, Doge, Bathilda, indeed everyone she mentions. Perhaps a thought is that there is something of the villain in everyone.

Politeness

The chapter is a great illustration of the lubricant of human interaction that is politeness. Harry and Hermione could very easily argue. They are physically and emotionally shattered after the events in Godric's Hollow. Harry's wand has been broken by Hermione's spell. Dumbledore appears to have left them without a guide for their quest, while Skeeter's poisonous book with its character assassination of Dumbledore has struck a raw nerve.

Hermione initiates a conversation with Harry with a polite opening: "Do you mind if I talk to you?" She uses this phrase because she knows Harry will mind, but notwithstanding she feels the conversation is important. The response from Harry is "No" but the authorial voice of Rowling tells us he says this "because he did not want to hurt her feelings.". The difficult conversation starts with Harry allowed by the language of politeness to feel that he is doing Hermione a favor, while of course she is the one helping him by holding the conversation. Politeness makes it possible.

Later Hermione tells Harry he is wrong. But again she does so in the language of politeness: "Harry, I'm sorry, but I think the real reason you're so angry …" Harry's response demonstrates his anger as he "bellowed," yet what he actually says is a measured agreement with Hermione's view: "Maybe I am!" Their emotionally charged exchange follows, with Harry's body language demonstrating emotional over-load, as he sits with his arms over his head, his voice "cracked with the strain." Hermione manages to make her point, keeping calm and making sure that Harry is in a position to hear it. Politeness wins.

The exchange is concluded with politeness. Harry switches to a triviality: "Thanks for the tea.".Within the context of the conversation we can interpret this as a broader thank you—it is also "thanks for saying what you have said.".It is also a closing device—Harry has heard all he can take at one go. And Rowling tells us that Hermione "recognized the dismissal."

The Secret Life of Severus Snape

Harry complains that Dumbledore has "left them to grope in the darkness." But Dumbledore hasn't! The guide he has left is Snape.

Since his betrayal of Lily and James Potter, Snape has worked unceasingly for the Order of the Phoenix and to assist Harry. He does this despite the loathing he feels for Harry, and which frequently erupts in his vindictive treatment and bad temper. Throughout *Harry Potter and the Deathly Hallows*, Snape acts consistently to help Harry. Without Snape it is hard to see how Voldemort would have been defeated—presumably not within the scope of this book anyway.

Snape receives no credit in his life for his action (save the respect of his friend Dumbledore) and even after his death his actions are not widely praised. Millions of Harry Potter fans regard Snape as the villain, and have not taken to heart Snape's role as guide throughout *Harry Potter and the Deathly Hallows*.

19. The Silver Doe

★★★★

Assessment

In the previous chapters readers have missed Ron. The great boost in this chapter is Ron's return. It is also a chapter when events go extremely well for Harry and friends. So far the success of the three has been limited to avoiding capture and recovering the locket—but not destroying it. Suddenly we have a chapter where everything goes well. At the end the horcrux is destroyed, the Sword of Gryffindor is in their keeping, and the three musketeers are once again three. It also becomes clear that someone is helping them, though they cannot guess who that someone is.

Re-Reading

The happy atmosphere of this chapter is strengthened on a second reading. That Harry was almost killed by the horcrux is almost forgotten, as are Ron's complex psychological hang-ups revealed when the locket tries to defend itself. The immersion in water at freezing point (fully dressed in Ron's case) could lead to a survival situation, yet this is pretty much glossed over. Indeed the chapter is summed up by Harry: "More than fine." The one who doesn't come off well in this chapter is Hermione, who falls into the role of a demented and screeching woman of an age before feminism was even thought of.

Heroes and Villains

The hero list is everyone in the chapter: certainly Ron and Harry, but also Snape who manages to find where they are and deliver the sword, and even Hermione who refrains from assaulting Ron.

Baptismal Washing

Rowling knows the canon of Western literature including the classics and the Bible. She must know that the total immersion in water experienced by both Harry and Ron has a sacramental value, whether perceived from a Christian standpoint or a mythical viewpoint. Harry plunges into the pool to retrieve a sword, a Christian symbol. Ron follows to save his life. Both are changed by the experience. Harry suddenly knows how to open the locket, allowing the evil it contains to be destroyed. Ron understands that the deeds Harry has done in the previous six years (which make him the hero and Ron the side-kick) sound "cooler" than they really were.

After this shared experience it seems impossible that Harry and Ron will ever argue again. I don't think they do in the book, although surely they must bicker in the years between Voldemort's defeat and the Epilogue.

The Secret Life of Severus Snape

Snape figures largely in this chapter, yet he is neither named nor recognized.

It is Hermione who says that she has brought them to the Forest of Dean; Phineas Nigellus overhears her and tells Snape; evidence that he is both aware of Snape's secret and that he is that rare thing, a modern-era Slytherin on the side of good. It is still a major task for Snape to locate them. First of all the Forest of Dean is a large area—it is in Gloucestershire, close to where Rowling grew up, and a place she probably knows well. Maybe Snape can guess that someone camping in the Forest of Dean will camp at an established tourist spot or even a designated campsite, and therefore reduce to a dozen or so the places to search. Yet of course Harry and Hermione have hidden their camp (as Snape knows they must, in order to evade Voldemort). His technique of showing a patronus is a clever one—though it assumes that Harry and Hermione will routinely keep a look-out at night, and also assumes that they will break cover in order to investigate. Snape is working hard to find them.

The patronus is a silver doe. Harry assumes that this cannot be dark magic or dangerous—yet we do see that Death Eaters cast patronuses, so his logic may be flawed; perhaps he assumes that the nature of the animal "patronized" suggests that it was produced by good magic. It is not made clear whether Harry knows that the patronus of his mother, Lily Potter, was a silver doe—but Snape cannot assume Harry doesn't know this as Sirius, Lupin, Mad Eye Moody or many others might have told him. Nor can Snape assume that neither Harry nor Hermione will know that a patronus can resemble that of a loved one. Harry of course knows of Snape's love for Lily. In short Snape risks being identified by his patronus.

In fact Snape's plan goes much as he wanted. He entices Harry from the camp—and he is lucky in getting Harry and Harry alone—and Harry sees the sword of Gryffindor in the pond where Snape has positioned it. Snape has placed the sword in a situation where it can only be recovered by action befitting a Gryffindor. Harry should be able to recover it with no greater problem than a plunge into water at freezing point. Of course it goes wrong because Harry is wearing the locket that is one of Voldemort's horcruxes, something Snape couldn't know.

The implicit plot is that Snape is watching from a little distance away; he therefore sees Harry submerge in the pool and sees him fail to resurface. Snape must be on the point of running to save his life when suddenly Ron appears and carries out the rescue.

The Coincidence of Ron's Appearance

Ron's arrival to save Harry is timed to the second. In part this is because he, like Harry, has been attracted by the Silver Doe, and only once Harry has left the camp can he see him. In a sense Ron saves Snape also, for had he not been there Snape would have had to break cover to save Harry and compromise his double agent status.

As far as the plot of the book goes the appearance of Ron at this time is pure chance. Yet it is such a big coincidence that it is possible to wonder whether Rowling considered linking in some way Snape and Ron's discovery of the location of Harry and Hermione. Ron uses Dumbledore's deluminator, whose manner of working is not properly set out. Probably Harry and Hermione need to say Ron's name for the gadget to work, yet the gadget seems to take Ron no closer than the general area where they are camped. Arguably the plot would be tidier if Snape had some input into the working of the deluminator so that he could program it with the information at his disposal.

20. Xenophilius Lovegood

Assessment

Xenophilius Lovegood comes across less as a character, more as a caricature. This is the strength and the weakness of the chapter. His first name means in Greek "lover of foreigners"; his surname is self explanatory. He is the good guy who sees the best in everyone, who is quirky, eccentric. These elements are made plain throughout the chapter, from the snippets of information we get about his home to the description of the man himself. Our attention is directed to the caricature.

Re-Reading

It is within this chapter that Lovegood makes the decision to inform the Death Eaters that Harry and friends are at his home. He knows that the likely outcome is the torture and murder of all three. Though it would not be Lovegood himself who does the torturing and the murder it is hard to take away the moral guilt.

Of course we can sympathize with his actions. Lovegood believes he may secure the release of his daughter. Yet his daughter is only imprisoned—to keep Lovegood from publishing a message Voldemort wants suppressed—while Harry and friends will be tortured and murdered.

Perhaps the kindest that can be said about Lovegood is that it was his foolishness that led to his daughter's kidnapping as a hostage, and now his foolishness to think he can somehow buy her freedom. I'm very close to saying that the only way his actions can be justified is if the reader feels he has lost his senses, or if the reader accepts that a parent is entitled to do *anything* to protect his child (arguably, Luna is in immediate peril for her life as long as she is imprisoned). His defense for the murder of Harry and friends might be the English one of "diminished responsibility". Maybe readers do feel well-disposed towards him—or maybe readers feel that Ron gets it right when he calls him "That treacherous old bleeder!" (chapter 22).

Heroes and Villains

Lovegood is of course the villain of the chapter. Yet Harry and friends exhibit a certain naivety. Arguably they are fools. They have plenty of experience of Voldemort's brutality, and surely should realize that Lovegood will be one of Voldemort's targets. The disheveled appearance of Lovegood should be a big clue that there is something wrong, but they don't spot it.

The Secret Life of Severus Snape

Snape must know that Luna has been kidnapped, as he is headmaster of Hogwarts and she is a pupil there. He is unable to do anything about this, as he is unable to do anything about much of Voldemort's evil.

21. The Tale of the Three Brothers

Assessment

This chapter struggles with a classic problem of narrative writing—how to tell a story within a story. *The Tale of the Three Brothers* is necessary to the plot of *Harry Potter and the Deathly Hallows*, but there is still awkwardness in its introduction into the story. Hermione reads it. But it's not clear who she is reading it to. Hermione has studied thoroughly all the stories in Dumbledore's bequest to her. Xenophilius Lovegood knows the story well. We are asked to believe that Harry and Ron have not read it, though this strains credulity as they have spent many months with Hermione trying to make sense of Dumbledore's task, and would surely have read the book which is part of the task. Anyway Ron knows the story, at least as told by his mum. As a plot device the reading of the story detains Harry and friends until the Death Eaters arrive—though on Tottenham Court Road earlier in the book the Death Eaters have demonstrated that they can move very rapidly, and in the circumstances a quick arrival of the Death Eaters would actually make more sense.

Re-Reading

The actual tale is superb. Here—and in *The Tales of Beedle the Bard*—we see Rowling as a twenty-first century fairy tale writer, producing new stories in this ancient genre. This tale is superb—

short, pithy, thought-provoking, even a guide to life. It is hard to praise it highly enough, and within the context of *The Tales of Beedle the Bard* it is superb. Notwithstanding within a Harry Potter novel it seems a poor fit.

Heroes and Villains

Lovegood's wrong action is protracted. It is not the case that he just made a momentary mistake in thinking he could trade three lives for the release of his daughter, but rather that he has reflection time while *The Tale of the Three Brothers* is read and does not change his mind. He might have told Harry and friends to flee.

The Secret Life of Severus Snape

Dumbledore wanted Snape to be the master of the wand that is one of the Deathly Hallows, and hoped that Snape would die undefeated and therefore that the power of the wand would die with him. We are not told whether he confides this in Snape. The plan is of course flawed. There is the flaw which is made explicit within the book—that it is Draco Malfoy, not Snape who defeats Dumbledore—and also the flaw that the most likely person to defeat Snape is Voldemort (the man who indeed kills him), a scenario that would lead the power of the wand to be transferred to Voldemort.

We are told that wizarding wills are made public, and we can assume that Snape will be familiar with the contents of Dumbledore's will, including the decision to bequeath *The Tales of Beedle the Bard* to Hermione. What we do not know is whether he makes any more sense of the bequest than does Hermione. Snape has himself worn Harry's invisibility cloak and is well placed to recognize this as the object alluded to in "The Tale of the Three Brothers." If Dumbledore has told him the true nature of his wand as another of the Hallows then he is well on the way to knowing about the Deathly Hallows.

It is possible to query Dumbledore's judgment. He is of course ultimately proved right in trusting Snape. Yet Dumbledore knows that Snape risks exposure to Voldemort and that potentially anything Dumbledore tells Snape may come to be learnt by Voldemort.

22. The Deathly Hallows

Assessment

By the time the reader gets to this stage in the book it is easy to grow weary of the scenario of Harry and friends camping out in hiding. The visit to Xenophilius Lovegood has resulted in near capture at the hands of the Death Eaters and a dramatic escape—and yet again we are back to camping out in hiding, somewhere in England.

Re-Reading

The chapter gives another example of the story-within-a-story format that occurs so frequently in this book. Here the inner story is provided by a radio broadcast. There's a lot of humor there, and the reader enjoys "spotting" characters we know from the earlier books in the series—but it still asks a lot of the reader.

The chapter has the same title as the book, and should perhaps therefore be pivotal. But I don't think it is! Harry considers chasing after the Deathly Hallows but of course later makes the decision to stick to Dumbledore's direction and seek the horcruxes. The chapter might be regarded as a bit of a dead-end.

Heroes and Villains

The radio broadcast presents a list of names of heroes who in ways large and small are fighting Voldemort's regime.

The Secret Life of Severus Snape

The radio programme "Potterwatch" presents Snape as a figure of fun. If someone moves quickly they move "faster than Severus Snape confronted with shampoo." Of course we laugh at Snape—yet if we stop to think about it for a moment this really isn't very nice. Ultimately Snape is shown to be the good guy, so perhaps we should regret laughing at him—yet I don't think we do.

Pedigrees. "Marvolo Gaunt said he was descended from the Peverells!" Pedigrees are a peculiarly British obsession, and something carried over into the magic world of Harry Potter. In the course of the seven books we learn quite a bit about the families of Harry, Ron, Sirius Black and even of Voldemort. That Marvolo Gaunt is indeed descended from the Peverells is significant because he inherited one of the deathly hallows—and because Voldemort feels a misplaced superiority because of his ancestry. That Harry is descended from one of the three brothers matters because this is why Harry has the invisibility cloak.

Rowling is interested in her own family and has been a subject of the BBC's *Who Do You Think You Are?* where a team of experts trace a celebrity's roots.

Wartime Radio reminds readers that sometimes the Harry Potter world seems to be in a time-warp. Today's teenagers are communicating through social networking using mobile devices.

Today's resistance to Voldemort would surely use Facebook, Twitter and Blackberry. Yet here we have a throw-back to the Second World War and the clandestine radio broadcasts.

For in the one part of the British Isles occupied by the Nazis—The Channel Islands—ownership of a radio was banned. To the Channel Islands and into occupied France the BBC sought to transmit clandestine programmes to aid the French Resistance and all the people of France. This is the world which Rowling appears to be imagining.

23. Malfoy Manor

★★★★

Assessment

On first reading this chapter is an adrenaline rush. A lot happens, it happens fast, it is surprising, shocking, violent, exhilarating. This is a real action-thriller chapter.

Re-Reading

A re-reading reveals the need for another re-reading! So much happens in this chapter that it needs a lot of attention. The meeting with Ollivander, Luna and Dean is unexpected. Dobby's arrival appears as if a *deus ex machina*, a God-sent angel who saves the day. Only much later in the story (chapter 28) do we learn how Dobby reached Malfoy Manor (and I suspect most readers miss this explanation).

Heroes and Villains

Many of the characters in this chapter endure suffering. Ollivander, Luna and Dean have been imprisoned and Ollivander has been tortured. Hermione is tortured in the course of the chapter. While we feel sympathy for them, this is different from regarding them as heroes. Dobby acts as we would expect a hero to act. Curiously so too does Draco Malfoy. He knows that identifying Harry and friends will lead to their torture and death and comes out with the incredible statement that he isn't sure.

The chapter has one clear villain in Bellatrix. She shares with Umbridge an enjoyment of torture. Rowling has created not one but two women who are simply evil.

The Secret Life of Severus Snape

Lucius Malfoy is confronted with the difficulty of identifying Harry, Ron and Hermione. Of course Draco should have no difficulty identifying them as he has shared classes with them for six years, but Draco prevaricates. The obvious solution for Malfoy is to call Snape, who would be able to make a firm identification. That he doesn't do this speaks volumes for how he regards Snape. As far as Malfoy is concerned, Snape is Voldemort's staunch ally, and to call him by mistake would be almost as bad as to call Voldemort himself. Additionally Malfoy wants to claim the credit for capturing Harry and his friends (in the hope that his past mistakes would be forgiven). Possibly he feels that Snape would claim the glory.

Good in Unexpected Places

Two of the bad guys act well in this chapter. First Draco Malfoy prevaricates when asked to identify Harry and his friends. He knows that Voldemort will torture them and murder them having himself seen Voldemort do this to others, and he avoids giving a firm identification. This certainly provides a delay, and without this delay it is most probable that Harry and friends would indeed have been murdered. In a sense Draco saves their lives. Draco shows that he is not a murderer. Dumbledore's work throughout

Harry Potter and the Half Blood Prince has been to keep Draco's soul unharmed. Draco certainly does things which are wrong and dangerous throughout that book and this, but he stops short of murder. Probably we are to infer that Draco's soul is still intact.

Peter Pettigrew's right action is momentary and subconscious. He delays by a fraction of a second the killing of Harry. Pettigrew has been presented throughout the novels as a weak character, the weak link in the Marauders group at Hogwarts (the group he was a member of with Harry's father James Potter, Sirius Black and Remus Lupin) and the weakest of Voldemort's followers. His life-time experience contrasts the kindness of the Hogwarts' Marauders with the brutality of Voldemort, while his life was saved by Harry's mercy in preventing Sirius Black from murdering him. Dumble-dore noted towards the end of *Harry Potter and the Prisoner of Azkaban* that Voldemort's servant was in Harry's debt. Here Petti-grew repays that debt by his hesitation. The immediate consequence is that he suffers a grotesque death strangled by the artificial hand Voldemort has made for him.

Pettigrew is throughout presented as a weak man used as a tool for evil rather than a man intrinsically evil. We are given no hint at the fate of Pettigrew's soul, yet perhaps there is hope that his final act of mercy will tip the balance in his favor.

24. The Wandmaker

Assessment

The sensitive reader will feel real grief on reading this chapter. Dobby has been a lovable figure in the books, and his murder is therefore a real cause of sadness.

Re-Reading

Harry's epitaph for Dobby is that he was "a Free Elf." In previous books in the series Hermione has made us all aware that the house elves are living in a state of servitude—in a nutshell they are slaves. It is Harry who frees Dobby from the Malfoys' oppression and Dumbledore who agrees that Dobby should have a contract of employment with a wage and holidays, key features of freedom. Dobby's death is not that of a slave required to undertake a life-threatening task—the sort of task Voldemort set for Kreacher—but the death of a free individual who through free choice acts bravely. No wonder #Dobby trended on Twitter!

Griphook comments that Harry is "an unusual wizard" because of the respect and grief he shows to Dobby. Our attention is drawn to the curious relationship between Harry and Dobby. Each have gone out of their way to help one another. By his death Dobby exemplifies "the love that pays the price", the ultimate sacrifice of an individual giving their life to save others. Harry later emulates Dobby's sacrifice.

Heroes and Villains

Dobby's death dominates this chapter, and his sacrifice makes him the undoubted hero. It also means that other characters perform well. In this chapter we see Harry using the task of digging by hand Dobby's grave as a way of showing his respect for Dobby's sacrifice. Luna uses a few, simple words to express the thanks of all for their deliverance from Malfoy Manor. Bill and Fleur accept their difficult and dangerous guests without a murmur of complaint. Griphook goes out of his way to compliment Harry. Ollivander does his best to help Harry. The magnificent act of heroism from Dobby brings out the hero in all it touches.

This is the chapter where Harry decides to put his energy into destroying horcruxes, not seeking out the hallows. He chooses to follow his duty as set out by Dumbledore over the lure of power presented by the hallows—an heroic decision.

Sacrifice is the theme of this chapter. Rowling might have written it with the words running through her head of Cecil Spring-Rice's *I Vow to thee my Country*, a British patriotic song sung to the tune of Gustav Holst's "Jupiter" from *The Planets*. The song is heard in the UK at every Remembrance Day, and was also played at the funeral of Princess Diana. Probably Rowling's school sang it —very many British schools in the 1970s and 1980s did.

Dobby makes the "final sacrifice" to save Harry and to help the good triumph over Voldemort's tyranny. His funeral demonstrates a clear belief in the afterlife (Luna's "I hope you're happy now") and with a cross marking the grave is within the Christian tradition. There is indeed "another country" for the gentle and peaceful soul of Dobby. His service to Harry is praised, but more important is his service to "another country" demonstrated by his "faithful heart".

I vow to thee, my country, all earthly things above,
Entire and whole and perfect, the service of my love;
The love that asks no question, the love that stands the test,
That lays upon the altar the dearest and the best;
The love that never falters, the love that pays the price,
The love that makes undaunted the final sacrifice.

And there's another country, I've heard of long ago,
Most dear to them that love her, most great to them that know;
We may not count her armies, we may not see her King;
Her fortress is a faithful heart, her pride is suffering;
And soul by soul and silently her shining bounds increase,
And her ways are ways of gentleness, and all her paths are peace.

25. Shell Cottage

Assessment

This is a grubby chapter. The negotiation with Griphook is not carried out in good faith. Ron clearly advocates double crossing him, and Harry's final deal is given with what is in effect a reservation in the small print—Harry will give Griphook the Sword of Gryffindor, but not when Griphook thinks

Re-Reading

The chapter improves little on re-reading. Harry, Ron and Hermione are not acting particularly well, while Griphook is presented in an unfavorable way.

The tone of the book changes from this chapter onwards. From this chapter onwards Harry is seeking horcruxes, not hallows. The pace of the action picks up as the months of camping out come to an end. Harry and friends go first to Gringotts, then to Hogwarts for the final showdown. It is possible that Rowling planned the book as three sections of twelve chapters each—here the putative third section starts.

Heroes and Villains

A grubby deal taints everyone. Griphook hardly shines—readers probably feel he should give his help unconditionally. Ron's willingness to advocate a straightforward break of promise doesn't reflect well on him. Harry's more subtle deception amounts to much the same. Hermione does not give leadership.

Perhaps a lesson for all readers is that it is very hard to maintain integrity. Perhaps also the lesson is that all should try harder. There is a contrast between this chapter and the one that precedes it. There everyone was a hero; here everyone is to some extent a villain.

Griphook

Griphook is presented in the same way as Shakespeare's Shylock, the Jew of Venice. Just as Shakespeare's audience knew little about Jews and lived in a society with only limited tolerance of Jewish people, so the wizarding world knows little about goblins but treats them with contempt. Shylock, like Griphook, is legalistic. Yes he will help Harry, but he demands his pound of flesh, the Sword of Gryffindor, and insists they shake on the contract. In Shakespeare's *Merchant of Venice* the contract between Shylock the Jew and the Merchant falls on a legal quibble—Shylock is judged to have the right to a pound of the Merchant's flesh but not a drop of his blood. Harry intends that the contract he makes should also fall on a quibble—the time of handover of the Sword of Gryffindor.

This really isn't nice. In Shakespeare, Shylock is presented as the villain and the audience rejoices that the contract cannot be carried out. Yet it is Shylock who is out of pocket on an agreement the

Merchant voluntarily entered into. Here Griphook will be out of pocket.

26. Gringotts

Assessment

In this chapter we're back to places familiar from the earlier Harry Potter novels—first the Leaky Cauldron, then Gringotts Bank. We also meet a dragon, a magical creature familiar from earlier books. This is all comfortable territory. Against this backdrop is a fast-paced, action adventure. Truly a satisfying chapter!

Re-Reading

There's a lot in this chapter! Some of the crucial plot details are covered with surprising brevity. For example Hermione can change into the shape of Bellatrix because one of Bellatrix's hairs is found on her jumper—this key plot element is found in parenthesis tucked into the first sentence. The chapter is particularly worth a careful re-reading because there are so many little details that contribute to the richness of the story.

Heroes and Villains

Harry and friends are of course heroes. Their raid on Gringotts is audacious, daring, perhaps fool-hardy, carried out with the sort of determination that readers have seen from this team in every one of the Harry Potter novels. This is Rowling at her most likable. "I've always been most impressed by bravery against the odds" (Rowling in BBC programme *Who Do You Think You Are?*). The actions of this chapter are indeed bravery against the odds, and Rowling seems most impressed with her own characters.

Griphook's behavior is more complex. He is certainly brave as he risks the ire of Voldemort. Additionally it is far from clear that the goblins would forgive a raid on Gringotts, even one made by a goblin with the intention of recovering a goblin treasure. These are real risks, yet Griphook's motivation for taking them seems to be nothing more than the acquisition of the Sword of Gryffindor, a motive which may seem to readers to be morally suspect. When they flee the Lestrange's vault his concern is only for the sword, not for the goblet that is the purpose of the theft, and he makes no effort to help Harry and friends. Possibly readers are to understand that Griphook and all goblins operate under a different value system. The topic is therefore one of intercultural value differences, and Griphook should be judged not by the value system of the world of Harry and friends but by the values of his culture. Maybe he is a hero.

The nameless dragon tends to win readers' approval. It has been tortured by the goblins, a circumstance which tends to make the goblins appear as villains. After years of captivity it seizes the chance of freedom and makes a daring escape. Surely all readers wish it well!

How different is the Magical World?

Rowling's magic world has obvious differences from ours. Harry and friends have broomsticks (not much in evidence in this book), wands, spells, instantaneous travel, a whole alternative technology that we don't have. But they also lack elements of our world. They don't have computers, mobile phones or iPads; there's no social networking and *The Tales of Beedle the Bard* are accessed as an old volume rather than an e-book. The technology is different but much is fundamentally the same. So how does Hermione protect her handbag from the snatchers? Does she use some amazing spell? No, she protects it by the low tech solution of stuffing it down her sock!

27. The Final Hiding Place

★★★★

Assessment

Hitching a ride on the back of a dragon is a superb, visual image—as is getting off by dropping feet-first into a lake. In what could be a bleak stretch of the book there's a bit of humor—Hermione's concern for the fate of the dragon for instance.

Re-Reading

The key information in the chapter, for more important than the theatre of the dragon ride, is that Voldemort realizes Harry and friends are chasing his horcruxes. It is Dumbledore's achievement that this has been hidden from him for two years, but now he knows the climax is inevitable. Harry also realizes the inevitability of a climax. He, Ron and Hermione are exhausted, yet there is no time to recover, sleep, tend their burns, plan—rather it is essential that they go to Hogwarts, and as they cannot directly enter the school that they go to Hogsmead and look for a way in.

Why so Short?

At around eight pages this chapter is half the length of the average for *Harry Potter and the Deathly Hallows*. Rowling clearly planned her books chapter-by-chapter, and the chapters tend to be of about the same length.

What we are seeing is a change of pace. Previously Harry and friends have planned their every move—the raid on the Ministry of Magic, the trip to Godric's Hollow, the visit to Lovegood, the theft from Gringotts. Each one of these escapades has developed in ways that they could not anticipate with the result that they make spur-of-the-moment decisions. Each one results in a desperate escape, twice from Death Eaters, once from Voldemort, once from the goblins at the bank—and always with the knowledge that capture will lead to torture and death. Now readers notice a change of pace. There is no planning around the events that lead to the Battle of Hogwarts, rather a determination to act as the moment dictates.

What is missing from this chapter is therefore the plan. There is no preparation.

Heroes and Villains

By this stage in the story Harry, Ron and Hermione are enduring events. Their escape by dragon is frightening and cold and ends with a plunge into freezing water; they are covered in burns and minor injuries. There is no particular act of heroism or villainy in the story as it affects these three.

Scotland is not named in this chapter, yet it seems clear that the dragon flies from London to Scotland. After leaving London it heads north, and as it doesn't come near a coast it seems it is flying along the backbone of England, the Pennine Chain. It comes to an area of deep-green mountains and lakes, and the lake that it finally settles on "did not seem to be very deep". Now of course the clues are scant. The only area of northern England with mountains and lakes is the Lake District of Cumbria, and these lakes are mostly well-known for their depth. Furthermore Rowling has not previously written about the Lake District. More likely would seem to be that Rowling intends the lake to be in Scotland. One that fits the description as a shallow lake with lots of reeds and mud is the southern end of Loch Lomond, a common day trip destination for people living in Scotland's Central Belt, including the city of Edinburgh where Rowling lived and wrote the Harry Potter novels. Just possibly the scene of this chapter is Scotland's Loch Lomond.

28. The Missing Mirror

Assessment

This chapter is too complicated. Aberforth presents a lot of information relating to many different parts of the story and indeed to different parts of the Harry Potter series. It is too much to take in, especially when readers are turning pages as quickly as possible to reach the climax of the story. The plot makes use of near-miraculous interventions not once but twice in just a few pages. It is amazing that Aberforth just happens to be there to help Harry and friends. It is amazing that the portrait-tunnel into Hogwarts exists.

Re-Reading

A leisurely re-reading does show that Aberforth's story makes sense and explains what would otherwise be plot holes. In particular this chapter explains the arrival of Dobby back in chapter twenty-three, avoiding what would otherwise be a plot hole. But it's still easy to miss! If you did, it is Aberforth who sent Dobby, though quite how he got the timing so perfect isn't really explained.

Readers are left with the coincidence of unexpected aid being offered to Harry and friends both here and back in Malfoy Manor. Maybe the message is indeed that "fortune favors the brave" (Terence). This chapter improves on re-reading.

Heroes and Villains

The villains of the chapter are the nameless Death Eaters who try to capture Harry and friends. Aberforth is candidate for the role of hero, yet his manner of life is such that he would never be recognized with a medal.

Living in a Corrupted World

In much of this book readers' attention is on those who are committed to one side or other in the battle between the supporters of the Order of the Phoenix and the supporters of Voldemort. The trip to Hogsmead gives a glimpse of the life of Aberforth, someone who has avoided both courses of action.

Hogsmead has a curfew, and seems not to be a particularly nice place to live in. Yet Aberforth—and doubtless hundreds of other citizens of Hogsmead—is fit and well, working and getting on with his life. His bar is now frequented by supporters of Voldemort, and they "traffic potions and poisons" there, with Aberforth turning a blind eye. Readers of the whole Harry Potter series will remember several examples of shady dealings in Hogsmead pubs prior to Voldemort taking power, so perhaps there's nothing different in this. Aberforth sets out his own response to the corrupt world in which he is living: "I keep my mouth shut."

However Rowling doesn't leave matters there. Aberforth may not be a hero of the Order of the Phoenix, but it turns out he does a lot of good things. When the need arises he makes the decision to hide Harry and friends, and makes it instantly and instinctively. Readers learn that he has been sending food to students at Hogwarts who are hiding within the school in the "Room of Requirement."He is a man who carries out many acts of kindness, many of them unacknowledged and even unnoticed. He is a model for living in a corrupt world for those of us who do not have the courage of a Harry Potter.

29. The Lost Diadem

★★★★

Assessment

This chapter is almost a page from www.friendsreunited.com. While the website helps us all catch up with old school friends, so this chapter is a reminder of our old friends from Hogwarts. The Harry Potter books have been read by a special generation of readers who have read through all seven books as they were published and whose own childhood corresponds with that of Harry and friends. We all want to know how our friends have been since we last met them.

Re-Reading

Dumbledore's Army are among Harry's most loyal supporters—the supporters he doesn't know he has and whose adulation he finds difficult. These Hogwarts students know the real Harry. Many have been in class with him, done detention with him, even shared the same dorm with him, so they really do know Harry warts and all. Yet they seem to have signed up to the myth of the "boy who lived." The situation is complex, well-written and thought provoking.

Heroes and Villains

They're all heroes! We want them to be heroes, they are acting well, and we happily grant them hero status.

Names

There are a lot of them in this chapter, and taken together they demonstrate Rowling's genius for names. There's nothing random about them. Take the following as a sample:

Neville Longbottom

Neville is upper-class English, a name which goes all the way back to the Norman Conquest. Longbottom is from the county of Yorkshire (there are quite a few surnames ending in –bottom, the Yorkshire word for a valley). Together they suggest a family that once owned a big part of Yorkshire.

Seamus Finnigan

Seamus is about as Irish as names come. So too is Finnigan—surnames ending in –an almost always are Irish. Together they suggest Irish and Catholic.

Lavender Brown

The surname Brown is one of the most common English surnames. Many parents try to balance a common surname with an unusual first name, and Lavender certainly is unusual. The whole name seems very English.

Terry Boot

Boot is a Nottinghamshire name, from England's East Midlands. Terry is well-established in England.

Ernie Macmillan

One of the few clearly Scottish surnames at the Scottish school of Hogwarts is Macmillan. Curiously Rowling has coupled it with a first name typical of England, suggesting that Ernie Macmillan may be from an English family of Scottish descent.

Anthony Goldstein

Goldstein has its origin in the London Jewish community, a community that has been in England for many hundreds of years and is an integral art of the social fabric of England. Add the first name used in its full form—Anthony not Tony—and the name suggests a scion of a family of London bankers.

Michael Corner

Corner can be an English surname, but it is also distinctive of Scotland's Orkney Isles and the neighboring county of Caithness. Michael is more common in Scotland than in England. Perhaps in Michael Corner we have one of the few Scots at Hogwarts.

The Patil twins, Padma and Parvati

The legacy of the British Empire has established this Indian surname in the British Isles. The first names are also from India, suggesting that the Patil twins are from a family with links to India within a generation or two.

Cho Chang

Most Chinese names in the British Isles have entered with families migrating from Hong Kong. The surname Chang is here positioned in British style as the last part of the name; in China the name would be written Chang Cho.

Lee Jordan

The surname Jordan is widespread in England, mainly southern England. The first name Lee was once considered to be an Irish name, but from the 1960s—Rowling's own generation—was increasingly used in England.

Rowling offers an abundance of names, most of them English. Hogwarts may be situated in Scotland (never actually stated, but there seems to be little doubt) but it educates magically gifted children from the whole of the British Isles and is the only such school in Britain. As the English are by far the largest group within the British Isles it is inevitable that English names will predominate. Rowling certainly reflects this, with a broad geographical range from England. Additionally she remembers the new British names from Asia.

Ravenclaw's Pass-Question

Q . "Which came first, the phoenix or the flame?"
A. "A circle has no beginning."

This version of the chicken and the egg question is answered with "circle", a neat answer though perhaps not an obvious one. The usual response to the conundrum of the chicken and the egg is that the question cannot be answered.

30. The Sacking of Severus Snape

★★★★

Assessment

Snape is the character we've loved to hate through seven Harry Potter books. He has variously been a mean teacher and an almost pantomime villain, a spiteful man with a vendetta against Harry, Dumbledore's murderer and finally one of Voldemort's henchmen. We want him sacked!

Re-Reading

Readers are so sure that Snape is the bad guy that they miss that he actually acts well in this chapter. It is worth a second read simply to spot this.

Heroes and Villains

Two surprises here. First of all the hero of the chapter is Severus Snape, because of the manner of his departure. He allows people to think badly of him, just as he has previously allowed them to think he was Dumbledore's enemy and Dumbledore's murderer. It is a form of bravery, and even of heroism. The villain of course is Harry Potter, who stoops to torture.

The Philosophy Bit

> Q. Where do vanished objects go?"
> A. "Into non-being, which is to say, everything."

What does this actually mean? Does it mean anything?

Rowling read French as part of her University of Exeter degree, and must have come across *L'Être et le néant* —"Being and Nothingness"—by Jean Paul Sartre. The very first chapter has the example of a vanished object—Pierre. Lets say we go to a café expecting to meet Pierre, but when we get there Pierre is not there. Instead of Pierre we find an absence of Pierre, which Sartre calls "non-being," just the term Rowling uses. For Sartre this is a state of nothingness—the vanished object goes into a state of nothingness, which we humans can nonetheless perceive. Of course this is the opposite of what Rowling—through McGonagall—suggest, for the answer in Harry Potter and the *Deathly Hallows* is that nothingness is everything.

It seems that Rowling read a lot more Sartre than just the first chapter. Sartre suggests that human existence—being—is in a vast ocean of nothingness. But our being can impose order on this nothingness—for example we can call it something like "spirit" or "consciousness." In a sense the nothing becomes everything. Complicated? Well that's existentialism.

Crucio!

Harry uses this unforgivable curse on Amycus when he spits in McGonagall's face. This is not right action. It lacks proportionality for the wrong done by Amycus—it is not "an eye for an eye"—and it is a form of torture, therefore outlawed by the international consensus of the Universal Declaration of Human Rights. The result is that Amycus "writhed," he is like a "drowning man" and he is "howling in pain" before he falls unconscious. Harry is in the wrong. Yet McGonagall calls him "gallant.". Maybe Harry in part realizes this himself as he is aware that he is feeling emotions like Bellatrix, but this theme is not developed. Rather we the reader are going along with Rowling to yield to the human pleasure of seeing our enemies suffer.

The Secret Life of Severus Snape

Snape finds McGonagall out and about in Hogwarts when she should be asleep, and intuits that Harry is around. Remember Snape is an accomplished *"legilimens"* and can probably read McGonagall's mind. He might also be aware that Voldemort is coming. He asks McGonagall if she has seen Harry, then goes on to say "Because if you have, I must insist …" We don't hear what Snape "must insist" because McGonagall attacks him. But remember his primary motive in life is to look after Lily Potter's son, to look after Harry, however much he detests him. Presumably Snape was willing at this time to do anything to help Harry. Maybe "I must insist you tell me where he is"—if Snape could find him he could help him.

The fight between McGonagall and Snape tells us much about Snape's intention. He defends himself from McGonagall's curse, but with a shield, not a retaliatory curse. When she attacks him with a ring of fire he turns it into a big, black snake. Readers will remember that in *Harry Potter and the Chamber of Secrets* the serpent that is conjured from a wand is relatively docile and readily listens to instructions from Harry. There is nothing to suggest that Snape's serpent is dangerous. Then Snape first hides behind a suit of armor, then flees. Snape is a very powerful wizard—if he wished he could surely beat McGonagall. He is called "coward", yet surely his decision to run is a form of bravery. He has lost his safe position as Hogwarts headmaster (which Voldemort won't like) and all but signed his own death certificate.

There is an intriguing idea that Snape may be a vampire. In Harry Potter and the Prisoner of Azkaban Snape tries to reveal that Lupin is a werewolf by setting the Defence Against the Dark Arts class unscheduled work on the identification of werewolves. Later when Snape finds that Harry has the Marauders' Map, and (wrongly) assumes that Lupin must have given it to him, Lupin says he needs to speak with Harry about his homework on vampires. This seems to silence Snape. There is a view that this is inexplicable unless Snape is a vampire and therefore that Lupin is threatening to tell Snape's secret. Snape can certainly go out in daylight, but maybe there is some potion that permits this to happen (just as there is a potion to stop a werewolf from becoming violent). It has to be said that there isn't a hint of proof for this theory anywhere in the novels … until now that is. Snape escapes by jumping through a window and transforming into a "huge, bat-like shape,"which seems very close to saying he turns into a bat. These two episodes in two novels suggest to me that Rowling at least considered making him a vampire. Maybe in seeking to understand the troubled character that is Snape's we should factor in that he is a vampire living without killing people. It helps explain his earlier allegiance to Voldemort, and makes his subsequent redemption all the more remarkable.

Family Life

The chapter is almost a cameo of family life. Central is the reconciliation—Percy comes back. The scene is brief: he says he was wrong and is forgiven. Here we see human beings acting at their best.

Ginny is the only one of the Weasley family who is not over seventeen—who is therefore not an adult. Yet protecting her by sending her home is not going to help her when her whole family are at Hogwarts and fighting. Perhaps the time comes when age rules do have to be bent. Ginny is not technically of age, yet circumstances demand that she grow up very quickly.

"You old besom!" is hardly a current insult, though an older generation in Scotland will understand it. This is what Amycus calls McGonagall. A besom is a broom made from a bundle of birch twigs, what we think of as a witches broom, the sort of broom the witch McGonagall would fly (and in the Harry Potter novels wizards also fly). But in the Scots dialect—and remember

McGonagall seems to be a Scot and Hogwarts seems to be in Scotland, though neither fact is quite made explicit—a besom is what the dialect dictionaries call a "low woman.". Dialect dictionary writers tend to be polite in their language—the word really means prostitute. Amycus goes on to spit in McGonagall's face. It seems that we are supposed to understand "you old besom!" as the terrible insult it is, not as a bit of archaic English charmingly revived.

31. The Battle of Hogwarts

Assessment

This is a long chapter full of action and incident. The battle is presented in an adult fashion. It is not a B-movie where the robbers can't shoot straight and the cops hit with every bullet but a real battle where real people get hurt. And the chapter leads up to the death of Fred Weasley.

Re-Reading

In the fog of battle Harry acts very well, with some assistance from Ron and Hermione. Malfoy, Crabbe and Goyle try to kill Harry, Ron and Hermione, yet Harry saves the lives of Malfoy and Goyle—with Hermione's help and Ron's acquiescence. Crabbe is killed through his own spell. The saving of Malfoy and Goyle could almost get lost in a busy chapter within a full book, yet it is a superb, practical example of the philosophy of loving one's enemy.

Heroes and Villains

Harry of course, also Ron and Hermione.

Malfoy and Goyle are saved from the flames, starting them on a Snape-like path of repentance. Readers see little of Goyle. Malfoy demonstrated at the end of *Harry Potter and the Half Blood Prince* that he was unable to murder a man in cold blood. At Malfoy

Manor his refusal to identify Harry and friends helps to save them. Fundamentally he is a decent guy.

> **Ye have heard** that it hath been said, Thou shalt love thy neighbor, and hate thine enemy. But I say unto you, Love your enemies, bless them that curse you, do good to them that hate you, and pray for them which despitefully use you, and persecute you; That ye may be the children of your Father which is in heaven: for he maketh his sun to rise on the evil and on the good, and sendeth rain on the just and on the unjust.
>
> *Matthew* V:43-45

32. The Elder Wand

Assessment

If any reader does not as a result of this chapter find themselves stretched on an emotional rack then they are not reading with sufficient attention. This is a powerful chapter. Deaths earlier in the Harry Potter novels have been followed by a period of grieving, yet the battle means there is no time to grieve for Fred Weasley. Readers feel Ron's anger, hate Voldemort, are fascinated by the gruesome death of Severus Snape. Readers hurt as they read.

Re-Reading

Even this dark chapter has its moments of fun. Professor Trelawney enters the fray using not her wand but a crystal ball which she drops over a banister onto the head of Fenrir Greyback. And it works! The giant spiders which appear seem to be almost comic threats (though readers of the earlier Harry Potter novels will know they are deadly.)

Heroes and Villains

By this stage in the book everyone readers encounter is either hero or villain. Outstanding is Snape, who dies as a brave man, a fitting end to the sixteen brave years of his life of atonement. Voldemort displays more villainy as he kills the man he believes to have been his closest ally.

Human Eye Color is variable across a limited range of colors, mostly browns and blues. As Snape dies he looks into Harry's eyes, and Rowling's authorial voice tells us "the green eyes found the black". Neither has a common eye color.

Within the terms of the novels the eye colors are significant. Harry's green eyes mark him out as magical. Many times we hear that they are the color of his mother's eyes, and it is this reminder of Lily Potter that matters to Snape. Snape's black eyes suggest a black character. Immediately before his death he is thinking about Harry and gives Harry the memories Harry needs; at death when he looks into Harry's eyes he is surely thinking of the woman he loved.

Green eyes are rare. They are found almost exclusively among northern Europeans (or people of northern European ethnicity), and mostly in the Nordic countries. In the British Isles, green eyes are sufficiently unusual to be noteworthy. Everywhere they are more common in women than men.

Black eyes do not exist. Never. No exceptions. Brown coloring can be very dark, but is always brown not black. Presumably Rowling is using a degree of artistic license in creating a sinister outward appearance for Snape. Notwithstanding it is a departure from her usual realism. Within the fiction written about vampires there are accounts of vampires having black eyes, and at this final moment in Snape's life readers are perhaps reminded of the idea that he may be a vampire or part-vampire. Rowling has said that she does not regard him as a vampire and maybe that should end the argument, yet characters in a novel can take on a life which exceeds that intended by their creator. If he isn't a vampire, why does he have inhuman black eyes? Of course the magical race whom Rowling tells us have black eyes are the goblins, but I don't think anyone would suggest Snape is part goblin. Would they?

33. The Prince's Tale

Assessment

Few authors could make a chapter such as this work—yet I think Rowling somehow manages it. With the action racing towards a climax we suddenly have a flashback. The time depth is considerable, right back to the childhood of Snape and of Harry's mother Lily. And the flashback is not to just to one time but to a selection of key episodes in Snape's life. It is not that Snape's life flashes before his eyes as he dies, but that his life flashes in front of every reader.

Re-Reading

The chapter works for readers who have both read and thought about the previous Harry Potter novels. It cannot work for readers trying to read this book in isolation. Rowling has loyal readers who have read and re-read every novel. We really are interested in the early life of Snape and of Harry's parents, of events around the time of Harry's parents' deaths, of events in the intervening years. It is the readers whose special interest makes this chapter fly.

Heroes and Villains

This is Snape's chapter. I don't think it can be said to excuse the wrong things he has done in his life, but it does perhaps explain them. Snape is aware of the extent of his wrong-doing and responds with a life of atonement. Snape is indeed the hero.

Perhaps the chapter shows us something about the villains in life. There is no single villain who derails Snape's life. Rather there are a lot of people who nudge him in the wrong direction. Petunia's jealousy of Lily's magical talent creates needless friction. At Hogwarts Snape is bullied—by James Potter and Sirius Black—and this bullying does him real harm. Remus Lupin fails to act to prevent the bullying. Hogwarts school allows bullying to continue. The rise of Voldemort engulfs a damaged Snape, though the young Snape comes into contact not with Voldemort but with the mass of more junior villains. The villains in Snape's life are lots of people who don't act particularly well, or who standby while others don't act well.

Flashback

Snape's memories take readers to a childhood incident that transforms the life of three children and which has enormous consequences.

Lily Evans has a skill that her sister Petunia does not share. Within the Harry Potter world it is magic; within our world it may be an aptitude for sport, a special talent, personality, intelligence or any other quality which might make one child different to another. Lily is unable to stop using this skill, though her mother has told her to hide it and Petunia finds it distressing. Severus's intervention is to tell Lily that her skill is special, while rejecting Petunia because she does not have the skill.

It should be a passing squabble among children. Yet it creates the driving forces in the characters of two.

- Lily is least marked by the encounter. She tries to resolve matters with her sister and she tends to reject Severus. She is not emotionally scarred by it.
- Severus has found in Lily the love of his life. She has the same magical skill that he has. His childhood before Hogwarts has been lonely and isolated, and it is Lily alone whom he feels is a friend. The great sadness for Severus is that he goes from loneliness to a childhood infatuation and then when his advances are rebuffed he is unable to move on. In the Harry Potter series readers see Ron experience an infatuation, but he moves on, finding that he loves Hermione. Severus is stuck. After Lily marries he continues to love her, and after her death his love continues. His love is the enduring love story of the Harry Potter world, born in a childhood encounter and continuing to his dying moment, yet it is an unrequited love. He uses his love both to protect Harry and to defeat Voldemort, turning it into a tool for his personal redemption. Love is for Severus is damaged by his childhood experience and his life seems most unhappy, yet he does transform it into something of value.

- Petunia is jealous of her sister. On the one hand she sees Lily as a "freak"; on the other she wants to copy Lily by going to the same school. Hogwarts is a school which selects children aged eleven on the basis of a special skill—magical ability—much as the UK grammar school system selects children on the basis of academic ability. The grammar school system receives criticism for just the sort of reasons that are implicit in this criticism of Hogwarts—it excludes children. Petunia is damaged by her jealousy and by her sense of exclusion. She goes on to live a "normal" life (the word Rowling uses to describe the Dursleys), denying the existence of the skills she does not possess. It is unfortunate that the death of Lily and the intervention of Dumbledore force her to adopt her nephew.

The repercussions of this childhood squabble are immense. Snape is led into the company of the Death Eaters and is complicit in the murder of the Potters—then works against Voldemort. It is hard to see whether he does more harm or good. Perhaps the logic of his penance is that he makes amends. Petunia becomes an abusive foster mother to Harry and a bad mother to her own son Dudley, though there is no real malice in her. She is simply a person damaged by her experiences. Readers don't see the effect of her year living in the magic world on her character—it would be nice to think she finds some sort of acceptance.

34. The Forest Again

Assessment

This is a great chapter. If the Harry Potter series has a claim to be great literature—and I think it does—this chapter is central to the assessment. Rowling consistently goes beyond the themes usually associated with literature for children, not shirking topics including death. Yet here she goes beyond the stock of most adult works of fiction. Harry Potter is not a victim, but a brave soul who faces certain death to save his friends. His love for his neighbor is so great that he can sacrifice himself.

Re-Reading

This chapter is short. There is very little clutter to distract the reader from the central message.

Harry is helped. Knowing that he is about to die he realizes the meaning of the riddle on the snitch that encases the resurrection stone. The statement "I open at the close" means "I open at the close of life, at death". Harry's parents support him, his God-father Sirius and his mentor Lupin. Their spirits walk with him.

Harry's one question is "childish." He asks "Does it hurt?" And the answer is that death doesn't hurt.

Heroes and Villains

Harry is hero.

Harry walks into the forest knowing that he will die. It is not that he knows that he might possibly die, but that he is certain that he will die. He does this because he realizes that he is himself a horcrux and that he must die to end the misery of Voldemort's reign. Harry allows himself to be killed to save his friends. His love for his friends is so great that to save them he will walk to his death.

There can be no greater act of heroism.

Voldemort

"I thought he would come" says Voldemort, thinking that Harry has not come. Voldemort understands Harry very well indeed, understands that Harry will indeed lay down his life for his friends. Voldemort understands the influence of love. It is all the sadder that he does not himself feel love.

> This is my commandment, That ye love one another, as I have loved you.
>
> Greater love hath no man than this, that a man lay down his life for his friends.
>
> *John* 15:12-13

35. King's Cross

★★★★★

Assessment

Harry is dead. He thinks he is dead and readers think he is dead. I suppose subsequently readers re-categorize it as a near-death experience, but for the moment we can set this aside. There have been plenty of deaths in the Harry Potter novels, and plenty of hints that there is life after death. Readers of the books see Sirius Black fall through the veil of death, hear the prayers for Dobby, see the ghosts of Hogwarts (who have died but not past over) and have even walked into the Forbidden Forest with Harry and the ghosts brought to life by the resurrection stone. We have had plenty of suggestions that death is not the end. Yet now we see a proof. Harry, the character we have most closely followed and whom Rowling's authorial voice is always the closest to, is now dead. Yet he is alive.

Re-Reading

This is not a vision of heaven. It is however a vision of the Pearly Gates. The idiom has been updated, so the Pearly Gates are King's Cross railway station, strangely clean, and to pass through these gates it is necessary to get on a train. Dumbledore has the role of a saint, here sent to speak with Harry.

Judgment has not yet happened. While Harry is not in heaven, Voldemort is not in hell. Yet Harry is in his own body, unscathed, and with his sight miraculously corrected so he doesn't need glasses. He arrives at King's Cross station naked, though clothes do appear, seemingly for his comfort. Voldemort by contrast is a "naked child … its skin raw and rough, flayed-looking … shuddering … unwanted … struggling for breath." Neither Harry nor Voldemort are actually dead. Dumbledore suggests that Harry might simply get on a train, in effect accept death, but suggests to him that he has a chance to end the evil of Voldemort's rule. Harry chooses life. Seemingly Voldemort does the same as he struggles to breathe.

Harry subsequently remembers his vision of King's Cross. Perhaps Voldemort does too.

Harry's final question to Dumbledore is one we all want to ask: "Is this real? Or has this been happening inside my head? Dumbledore's answer—which is of course Rowling's answer—is profound. "Of course it is happening inside your head … but why on earth should that mean it is not real?"

Heroes and Villains

It would be presumptuous to say who are the heroes and who the villains. This chapter takes us to the Pearly Gates. Life is over; deeds of heroism and villainy, love and hate, good and ill, everything that can be done in life has been done. Onwards is the judgment.

36. The Flaw in the Plan

★★★★

Assessment

Rowling presents one assessment of this chapter through the mouthpiece of the Hogwarts' ghost Peeves:

> "We did it, we bashed them, wee Potter's the One,
> And Voldy's gone mouldy, so now let's have fun!"

Re-Reading

Harry's conversation with Voldemort sets out the flaw in Dumbledore's great plan, and the amazing way in which a chance series of events have repaired the flaw. In case readers miss the key steps in the argument they are as follows:

- Snape was "Dumbledore's man" from the time that Voldemort killed Lily Potter, because Snape loved Lily. Dumbledore planned that Snape should become the master of the elder wand.
- Shortly before his death, Dumbledore was overpowered by Draco Malfoy, who became the master of the elder wand—an unanticipated event.
- Snape killed Dumbledore on Dumbledore's instructions. Dumbledore's plan had been that in this way the power of the elder wand should pass to Snape. However the plan

went wrong because Dumbledore was no-longer the wand's master.

- Harry overpowered Draco, becoming the master of the elder wand.
- Voldemort is therefore trying to fight Harry with a wand which acknowledges not Voldemort but Harry as its master.
- In the duel the wand turns Voldemort's first curse back on Voldemort, and delivers itself to Harry. In effect Voldemort kills himself.

If Dumbledore's plan had worked as he intended then Snape would have become master of the elder wand. However Voldemort's murder of Snape would have made Voldemort the master. The final duel would have put Harry against the most powerful magician aided by an unbeatable wand—and it is hard to imagine the plot that on this scenario could have led to Harry's victory.

Heroes and Villains

Of course Harry is the hero, but there's another hero in this chapter—Voldemort. He is the anti-hero.

Harry is fresh from a near-death experience. His personal battle is won. It may be that Voldemort will kill him, but he now knows what will happen to him after death. He has little to fear from death. By contrast Voldemort has much to fear. His life has been spent in trying to avoid death. For many years he has secured his life through the horcruxes produced through evil magic, and he knows from experience that these work and that he cannot be killed while they survive. Yet in the previous few hours he has discovered that all his horcruxes have been destroyed and realized that he can now be killed. Like Harry he has had a near-death experience and it may be that he has an idea of the misery that awaits him. He also knows that the very wand he is using accepts Harry as its master. He knows that he will probably lose and he may even know that the consequence for him is an eternity of misery. It appears that in his final moments he accepts his fate, and in this acceptance there is a degree of heroism.

John Milton in *Paradise Lost* presents a vision of the devil in hell. Generations of students have found the devil to act like a hero, enduring the torments he faces. Voldemort appears in the camp of an anti-hero such as Milton's devil.

The Fate of Voldemort

Harry suggests that Voldemort should try to feel remorse for what he has done, the one thing that has a chance of putting back together his split soul. The statement hits home—Voldemort is "shocked" and his hand is "trembling."

Voldemort's penultimate words are a threat to kill two people: "… after I have killed you, I can attend to Draco Malfoy". His final words are the killing curse "Avada Kedavra!" If he has understood

Harry's explanation of the flaw in the plan (as surely he must) then he knows he must lose this duel. Starting to fight is a form of suicide. It is fitting that it is his own curse that turns against him. Harry cannot be said to kill him

Voldemort has lost his human identity as Tom Riddle by splitting his soul in seven. In his final moments he has been unable to feel remorse for what he has done, threatened two murders and in effect killed himself. The future of his soul appears to be that which readers have seen for a fragment of his soul in Harry's vision of King's Cross. While Dumbledore points out to Harry that Harry has little to fear from death, Voldemort it seems has much to fear.

Epilogue—Nineteen Years Later

★★★★

In a few pages we are introduced to the next generation:

The Potter Children:

James Potter

Albus Severus Potter

Lily Potter

The Weasley Children:

Rose Weasley

Hugo Weasley

Draco Malfoy's Son:

Scorpius Malfoy

We have the cast for what should be the next novel.

> "The scar had not pained Harry for nineteen years. All was well."

Can any reader believe that Rowling penned these final words without thinking of the next book? Everyone knows that it is just when everything is well that disaster strikes. Surely in the next chapter Harry's scar should pain. Surely there should be a story where the Harry and Hermione of the next generation—Albus Potter and Rose Weasley—should be set against the Draco of this new generation—Scorpius Malfoy? Or perhaps in a twist Albus, Rose and Scorpius could all be friends. Could they all three be in Slytherin?

The elder wand still exists, in Dumbledore's grave. The resurrection stone is somewhere on the ground in the Forbidden Forest. Harry still has his cloak of invisibility. Therefore all three hallows exist and there is the possibility that they will be reunited. Voldemort is surely dead—but another dark wizard may arise.

I rather wish Rowling had kept writing.

A Note of the Deaths

A staggering number of people die in this book. Of course many books for children and young readers do include deaths, but almost none in this profusion. Perhaps children of a past generation would have been reading the *Old Testament* and found deaths aplenty there, many pretty gruesome, but for books specifically written with child readers in mind the body count does seem high, while almost all meet a violent end.

THE DECEASED	THE KILLER	MANNER OF DEATH
Cadmus Peverell	suicide	poison (however hung in the film version)
Antioch Peverell	A murderer	his throat is slit
Ignotus Peverell	None, in effect old age	natural causes
The Grey Lady	The Bloody Baron	stabbed
The Bloody Baron	suicide	stabbed
Percival Dumbledore	unknown (in Azkaban)	unknown
Kendra Dumbledore	Ariana Dumbledore	accidentally killed
Ariana Dumbledore	Albus Dumbledore, Aberforth Dumbledore or Gellert Grindelwald	accidentally killed
Regulus Black	Inferi commanded by Voldemort	drowned

Table 1: Those who Died Before the Time of the Book.

Of the nine who died before the time of the book, seven are killed, one died as a result of suicide (Cadmus Peverell) and just one of natural causes (Ignotus Peverell).

THE DECEASED	THE KILLER	MANNER OF DEATH
Charity Burbage	Voldemort	killing curse
Mad-Eye Moody	Voldemort	unknown
Rufus Scrimgeour	Pius Thicknesse (under the imperius curse cast by Yaxley)	presumably killing curse
German woman	Voldemort	killing curse
German child (1)	Voldemort	killing curse
German child (2)	Voldemort	killing curse
Gregorovitch	Voldemort	presumably killing curse
Gellert Grindelwald	Voldemort	presumably killing curse
Bathilda Bagshot	implied killed by Nagini	presumably eaten by snake
Ted Tonks	Snatchers	unknown
Dirk Cresswell	Snatchers	unknown
Gornuk	Snatchers	unknown
Peter Pettigrew	Voldemort	strangulation by artificial hand
Dobby	Bellatrix Lestrange	thrown knife
Vincent Crabbe	accidental death	fiendfyre
Fred Weasley	presumably by Augustus Rookwood	blown up
Remus Lupin	Antonin Dolohov	unknown
Nymphadora Lupin (Tonks)	Bellatrix Lestrange	unknown
Colin Creevey	unknown	killed in battle
Severus Snape	Nagini (ordered by Voldemort)	Snake bite

Bellatrix Lestrange	Molly Weasley	Unclear, presumably killing curse
Voldemort	himself	own killing curse rebounds

Table 2. Named Characters Killed During the Book.

This is a total of twenty-two deaths, all violent. Vincent Crabbe's death is accidental, though in the context of a fight, but all are the others are killings.

In addition there is mention of an unidentified fallen fifty of the Battle of Hogwarts, all killed by violent means, and implicitly additional to the deaths we know about.

Harry Potter and the Deathly Hallows therefore contains 81 deaths, all but one violent. Additionally two named animals are killed. Hedwig (Harry Potter's owl) is killed by a Death Eater's spell on the flight from Privet Drive. The killing curse was presumably aimed at Hagrid but missed. Nagini, Voldemort's snake, is killed by Neville Longbottom by being decapitate using the sword of Gryffindor.

Is Harry Potter Christian?

An area that has bothered critics of the first six Harry Potter books is how they fit with Christianity. There is certainly a view that books which deal with magic, witchcraft and wizardry are not Christian.

Many critics and readers have resolved the issue by pointing out that the Harry Potter novels are using magic as an alternative technology, just as does the genre of science fiction. Indeed they fit the bookshop category of “science fiction and fantasy” rather than “occult” In an occult story characters draw magical powers from the devil—a genre with Marlowe’s play *Dr Faustus* as one of the early examples, where the hero makes a pact with the devil and is ultimately dragged off to hell. By contrast in fantasy the magical powers are simply skills or abilities which characters possess. Harry Potter falls clearly in the fantasy group.

A key feature of the final Harry Potter novel is that a Christian context is brought into the foreground. Readers see that Harry and friends live in a world which is culturally Christian. There are all sorts of hints of this, for example:

- The inscription on Harry Potter’s parents’ grave is from the Bible: "The last enemy that shall be destroyed is death" (*1 Corinthians* 15:26).

- On Dumbledore's grave there is also a Bible quote: "Where your treasure is, there your heart will be also" (*Matthew* 6:21).
- Harry uses a cross as a grave-marker when he buries Mad Eye's artificial eye.
- Harry becomes God-father to Lupin and Tonks's son.

In addition to living in a world which is culturally Christian, Harry acts as a Christian. Two issues are outstanding:

- He is prepared to die so that his friends can live.
- He encourages Voldemort to seek redemption through remorse.

While Harry is the outstanding example of a Christian lifestyle, he is certainly not alone. Dumbledore's willingness to die to save Draco's soul is a Christian act, as it Snape's life of atonement for a wrong he did. Very many characters in the book act in a Christian fashion.

The case for regarding *Harry Potter and the Deathly Hallows* as an outstanding Christian novel is in my view overwhelming. And against this background it is all the more surprising that the Christian backlash continues. A possible reason is given by Jerry Bowyer, an American radio and television host for public affairs and politics:

> "So much of the religious right failed to see the Christianity in thc Potter novels because it knows so little

> Christianity itself. Yes, there are a few 'memory verses' from Saint Paul, and various evangelical habits like the 'sinner's prayer' and the altar call. The gospel stories themselves, the various metaphors and figures of the Law and the Prophets, and their echoes down through the past two millennia of Christian literature and art are largely unknown to vast swaths of American Christendom".
>
> Jerry Bowyer. *Harry Potter and the Fire breathing Fundamentalists* www.townhall.com 2nd August 2007.

Those in doubt about the Christianity of the Harry Potter novels and the example set by Harry Potter may care to look at his actions within the context of the following key Bible quotes:

- Greater love hath no man than this, that a man lay down his life for his friends. *John* 15:13
- "I am the good shepherd. The good shepherd lays down his life for the sheep. *John* 10:11
- This is how we know what love is: Jesus Christ laid down his life for us. And we ought to lay down our lives for our brothers. *John* 3:16

The Harry Potter novels are stories of Christianity in action with Harry Potter as a Christian hero.

Publishing Information

Nimble Books LLC
1521 Martha Avenue
Ann Arbor, MI, USA 48103
http://www.NimbleBooks.com
wfz@nimblebooks.com
+1.734-330-2593

Revision number 92; last saved 06/11/12
Printed in the United States of America
ISBN-13: 978-1-60888-138-3

∞ The paper used in print versions of this publication meets the minimum requirements of the American National Standard for Information Sciences—Permanence of Paper for Printed Library Materials, ANSI Z39.48-1992. The paper is acid-free and lignin-free.

www.ingramcontent.com/pod-product-compliance
Lightning Source LLC
Chambersburg PA
CBHW060619310726
48982CB00003B/610

* 9 7 8 1 6 0 8 8 8 1 3 8 3 *